GHADY & RAWAN

EMERGING VOICES IN THE MIDDLE EAST

Series Editor
Dena Afrasiabi

Other titles in the series include:

Dying in a Mother Tongue (2018) by Roja Chamankar

Using Life (2017) by Ahmed Naji

Limbo Beirut (2016) by Hilal Chouman

A Bit of Air (2012) by Walid Taher

I Want to Get Married! (2010) by Ghada Abdel Aal

Ghady
&
Rawan

Fatima Sharafeddine and Samar Mahfouz Barraj

Translated by **Sawad Hussain** *and* **M. Lynx Qualey**

CENTER FOR MIDDLE EASTERN STUDIES
The University of Texas at Austin

Library of Congress Control Number: 2019935331
ISBN: 978-1-4773-1852-2

Translated from Fatima Sharafeddine & Samar Mahfouz Barraj, *Ghadi wa Ruwan.*
Dar al saqi, Beirut, 2014.

Cover design by Samantha Strohmeyer
Book design by Allen Griffith of Eye 4 Design

CONTENTS

CONTENTS

GHADY & RAWAN

GOODBYE, SUMMER

THE LIGHTS GO OUT in the apartment and everyone goes to sleep, but Ghady's eyes stay open, refusing to surrender to the end of the day. He knows exactly why he's flooded with worry. It isn't the first time, and it definitely won't be the last.

The days here flew by so fast! But summers in Lebanon are always like that. As soon as one summer ends, Ghady starts the countdown to the next. And every year, like today, he feels sad. Just a few more days, and he'll be starting school in Brussels, the city where he moved when he was three years old.

"What are you dreaming about? Come on, we're here." His sister Zeina shakes him by the shoulders to get him to open the car door and make room for her to get out. Ghady says nothing. He steps out, slings on his Eastpak, and drags his suitcase behind him, following his parents. He walks beside his cousin Jad, who has come along to say goodbye.

Back at the house, while saying goodbye to his grandparents, Ghady had held back tears. Now, when the time comes to part, he avoids Jad's hug. Ghady pulls away, waving as if he'll be back shortly. "Bye. See you soon!"

The wheels on the plane speed up, and the roaring of the engines grows louder, putting pressure on Ghady's already strained nerves and on the tears he's been trying to hold back. When they leave the ground, his heart sinks, and with the power of the plane's takeoff he feels a hot, thick stream of tears break loose against his will, running free. He can't control it. He sticks his face right up against the small window so his mom won't see him crying, and he sees Beirut recede farther and farther away until it becomes a speck on the horizon, then disappears. The plane glides over the sea, its shadow reflecting on the calm watery surface below. No waves . . . . Waves are only by the shore, and by now the shore is far away.

Ghady leans back against his headrest. He closes his eyes and thinks of Jad and Rawan, his grandparents' neighbor. Ghady only sees Rawan during these yearly trips to Beirut, but they are really close friends. Yesterday, Rawan invited him and Jad to spend the day with her family in the mountains. He had so much fun out there that he forgot about his rapidly-approaching departure. They didn't ride bikes like they usually did, and they didn't climb to the top of the mountain behind the house. Instead, they spent hours in the treehouse that Rawan's father had built in the crown of a huge walnut tree. The treehouse was the only place where they could talk freely without Rani, Rawan's older brother, annoying them with his sarcastic comments. They had laughed so much at Jad's hilarious jokes, and at Rawan, who had brought grapes up and dropped them onto the heads of the adults sitting below.

Now, Ghady thinks about how much he will miss his friend between now and his next summer visit. He pulls at his shirt collar and stretches it up toward his face, wiping the tears. When he's sure he has gotten rid of any evidence of crying, he turns to his mother. "Mom, when are we coming back to Beirut?"

She chuckles. "Are you missing it already? We'll be back in about ten months."

Ghady quickly counts up the days. "That means . . . after 300 days?"

"Just about," his mother answers, preoccupied with reading a magazine she has plucked from the seat pocket in front of her.

"Don't forget to book the tickets when we get back to Brussels."

"Sure thing, Sir."

The plane rises above the clouds and the turbulence stops, allowing the flight attendants to offer the passengers food and drinks. Ghady heaves a huge sigh. His nerves are calmer now that he's cried and vented his frustrations after the end of a trip he enjoyed from start to finish.

"I'm starving," he says.

"You're always starving," Zeina retorts from the seat behind him. She also has a window seat, next to their father.

"Spare me your stupid comments," Ghady snaps. "Why don't you just put your headphones back on."

"You're the stupid one. Why are you being so mean?"

Ghady knows what he said to his sister was over the top. In truth, he envies Zeina's attitude. Unlike him, she is happy to go back to her own room and bed after two months of chaos, when she wasn't able to shut herself away in their grandparents' home. She likes reading and listening to music, and she needs time alone, without interruptions. That doesn't mean she doesn't have fun during their summer visits to Lebanon—especially when their mom lets her go out at night with older cousins, or when she spends a few days with them in the south, in a cabin on the beach.

Ghady cheers up as soon as he gets busy eating everything on the tray in front of him. He leaves nothing, not even his mother's untouched dessert.

He draws a book from his black backpack, which he'd flung between his feet, and starts reading. "This will make the time go faster, and that way I won't get too bored on the plane," he says, not expecting his mother to answer. He knows that when she's absorbed in reading, she won't hear anything around her.

After a while, his eyelids begin to droop. The book slides from his hands, and he turns his head and rests it on his mother's shoulder, dozing off.

Ghady doesn't wake up until a hand ruffles his long ringlets and whispers in his ear, "Come on, wake up sweetie, we're here."

Ghady wakes with a start and remembers: he's in Brussels. Oh well, it would do for now. He no longer feels down. Instead, he's excited about going back to the house, to his things, his video games, after such a long time away.

3

THE EMPTY BALCONY

THE PHONE IS RINGING, each ring louder than the last.

Almost every room in the house has a phone, and every phone has its own ringtone. Rawan listens to this strange symphony, and her mind wanders as she gazes at the sapphire sky outside her window and snuggles up between her pillow and duvet. Looking at her clock, she thinks, *Ghady's plane must have taken off by now.*

"Someone pick up the phone!" Rawan's mother yells. "Rawan, can't you hear it ringing? I'm busy in the kitchen and my hands are dirty! Hurry and pick it up!"

Rawan rolls out of bed, grumbling. "Ouff . . . what is this? Rawan do this, Rawan do that! It's always *Rawan* who has to pick up the phone. I don't get it! Why wasn't I told I'd been appointed Guardian of the Phones in this house? Anyway Mama, I'm sure this call is from one of Mr. Rani's friends or admirers, or else it's Nawal next door who's always asking you about some recipe. Why doesn't she just buy a cookbook and leave us in peace? I mean, no one ever calls me on the house phone!"

Rawan picks up the receiver, irritated. "Hello? Yes? . . . Oh. . . . Hi, Jad. How are you? . . . Really? Well . . . thanks for calling. Why didn't you call me on my cell, like usual?" She raises her voice so whoever is at home can hear. "Ah . . . Well, seems like it needs a charge. Catch you later."

Her brother Rani pokes his head out from his room and mimics her voice: "I mean, no one ever calls *me* on the house phone . . ." She cuts him off angrily. "Argh, Rani! You're lucky this time, but next time this annoying phone rings, I won't answer if it's for you. Trust me, if I see one of your friends' numbers on the caller ID, I won't pick up. I've memorized all their numbers from their billions of calls!"

Rawan makes her way to the sitting room, thinking about what Jad has just told her: "Ghady says hi. He says he really misses us already, and that he's counting the days until he sees us again."

Rawan stands at the window and looks out at the fourth-floor balcony of the building across the street. The balcony looks empty and sad, even though its pots are bursting with colorful flowers and leafy plants. Ghady's gone, and she won't see him standing there again for a long time. Ghady used to look out every morning from that very balcony: He'd wave at her and give a short whistle, announcing a new day of fun and adventure. That whistle was a signal for them to meet up at the field behind the building, where they'd get together with Jad and a group of neighborhood kids.

Now, Rawan feels glum. During the summer vacation, she had so much fun, giggling with Ghady and Jad in a way she didn't the rest of the year. She's already bored, and Ghady has been gone only a few hours. Having Jad nearby won't fill the emptiness she feels in her heart. The three of them make up "The Three Musketeers," as their families call them. But it's different without Ghady, the friend who understands her and who lets her be her true and complete self. Rawan steps into the kitchen. She eats a banana. She drinks a glass of juice and, without thinking, gulps a glass of water straight after. She doesn't realize what she's done until she feels the uncomfortable swelling in her stomach. She goes back to the living room and sprawls out on the couch, turns on the TV for a few minutes, and turns it off. Then she makes her way back to her room. She waters the plant on her windowsill and stands in front of the mirror.

Rawan contemplates her face and her long, silky, wavy hair. She grins. She remembers what Ghady told her at the start of the summer. "Rawan, you look really nice with long hair. It looks like the waves on the sea . . . Don't ever cut it, or I'll call you 'Rawan the lamb'."

She draws closer to the mirror and discovers a few small pimples ready to blossom again on her forehead. That's how she sees and imagines them, as tiny flower buds. She always tries to see things differently, like you would in a cartoon, in the "Rawan way," as her friends call it.

She heads to the bathroom and washes her face with a special soap for getting rid of those tiny buds, which are preparing to adorn her beautiful face. As she dries her face with a towel, she thinks, *If only things were better in Lebanon! Then Ghady's parents would come back here to work, and they wouldn't be forced to work in Belgium and take my best friend with them. It would be so great if they were here all the time! But I don't understand why Ghady doesn't like living there. I mean, life in Belgium must be tons easier than life over here. He's super lucky.*

BRUSSELS

GHADY AND HIS FAMILY find the taxi driver waiting for them—the same driver who meets them after every trip. Ghady's dad always asks this driver for a ride to the airport at the start of the summer, and for a pickup when they get back to Brussels at their vacation's end.

The arrivals hall here is so different from the one in Beirut! When Ghady gets to the airport in Beirut, Jad and Rawan are always waiting, even if he lands at one or two in the morning. Here, in Zaventem Airport, the taxi driver is the only familiar face . . . There's no friend, no cousin . . . Ghady has friends here in Brussels, sure, but it's different. They aren't in touch over summer vacation, since everyone is busy with themselves and their own things.

It's raining as Ghady walks with his family to the parking lot. *I almost forgot how many more rainy days there are in this city,* he thinks.

"Brussels welcomes us!" Ghady's dad says, laughing.

"I love walking in the rain," Zeina says. "I've missed it."

Ghady doesn't say anything. He just closes his eyes and lifts his face to the sky, as if it could wash away the longing that rises up inside him at the sound of raindrops pinging on the roofs of the cars.

Each of them drags a bag or two, following the walkway—except Ghady's mom, who runs to the car, trying to escape the rain by huddling beneath her purse. The driver puts the bags in the trunk as they settle in the car, water dripping from their hair and the tips of their noses. They close the doors, and the car starts up.

Ghady looks out the window. "What a change!" he says aloud, and Zeina asks, "What are you talking about?" He doesn't answer, just nods his head toward the outdoors.

"Ohh," she says. "You mean the roads and the street signs? Or how clean everything is? How it's so calm and orderly?"

He nods.

His mom laughs. "See? There are good things about living here."

"Yes, but Ghady doesn't see them! It's not like Lebanon, the *love* of his *life*," Zeina says to annoy her brother.

Ghady's face flushes tomato red. "You don't understand anything! Rawan is my friend. Just a friend! Dad, tell Zeina to stop being such a brat!"

Their dad turns from his place in the front seat. "Don't get so angry, bud. And you, Zeina, leave your brother alone."

Silence returns, and Ghady goes back to thinking about Lebanon and his friends there. This time, he forces himself to hold back his tears. Not now, because Zeina will show no mercy. She'll definitely attack if she sees tears. Plus, his parents will be worried.

At home, Ghady runs to his room to make sure his stuff and his video games are all where he left them. Then he remembers the letter and opens his bag. Rawan wrote it, asking him not to read it until he got home. He pulls out the paper, which has been folded twenty times, from the inside pocket of his bag.

Wednesday, September 3, 2008

My friend Ghady,

When you read this, you'll be far away, and I'll have started to miss you. We had so many fun summer days! No school and no homework. We partied a lot and slept till noon, visited friends, swam, played volleyball at the club . . . Now you're gone, and soon school is going to start. Then we'll be back to classes and brutal exams . . .

Oh Ghady, you're so lucky you live in Europe. Everything there is so well-organized, plus you have so many green spaces and fast internet. I'm so jealous. I wish I could leave Lebanon and live in a country like Belgium. I wish I could study in a school like yours, where there are no heartless exams . . .

I hope this year is fun for both of us, and that it goes by super fast. Write to me sometimes. Don't forget about your friends in Beirut!

Best,
Rawan

After Ghady reads the letter, longing surges back into his heart. Why is life like this? Is his family ever going to move back to Lebanon? Rawan is definitely exaggerating about how hard the schools are. He'd be so happy there, and his classes would be easy.

He decides to turn on his computer and send her a message.

Wednesday, September 3, 2008

My friend,
This city is cold and empty. Seriously, Rawan, there's a huge difference between Beirut and Brussels. Ahh! I want to come back to you on the same plane, which is probably still parked in the same spot at the airport. I don't want to be here. The noise of the Beirut streets, with all its car horns, is better than the silence here. I'm happy to be back in our house, though. Honestly, I missed my comfy bed and a room that no one comes into without knocking. And hey, when I got here and read your letter, I felt like you were with me. So thanks.

Tell Jad I said hi. (I know he hates to write letters.)

Best,
Ghady

GETTING READY

"MAMA, TELL RANI to get out of the bathroom! He's
not answering me. And he's been in there for seriously at least half an
hour!" Rawan calls. "This is unbelievable! He changes his clothes in the
bathroom, he reads magazines in the bathroom, he talks on his phone
in the bathroom . . . not to mention the cologne he sprays on every day,
which I swear is giving me an allergic reaction. He thinks girls are going
to follow him just like in the ads. Pathetic!" She lets out a shout of rage
and pounds on the door. "Rani! Get out of there—and fast! This isn't
your private bathroom!"

Rani opens the door and walks out in a cloud of overpowering
cologne. As soon as it hits Rawan, she starts to cough and sneeze. Tears
stream out of her eyes, and she asks: "What is this cologne even called?
Insect repellent smells better. Have mercy! Why can't you do it in your
room?"

"The mirror's bigger in here and the light's better. It's way too dark
in my room and my mirror doesn't do the trick. Next time *you're* in the
bathroom, let's set a timer and see who's in there longer." Rani says as
he swaggers to his bedroom.

Rawan's mother comes up. "Calm down, Rawan. Can't you stop this
ridiculous bickering with Rani? You're brother and sister. This isn't how
siblings treat each other. Besides, you *do* spend a lot of time in the
bathroom."

Rawan's mother turns to go back to the living room. She stops for a
moment in front of Rawan's bedroom door, which is open, and steps

10

in to look around. Rawan watches her facial expressions and braces herself for what's coming. *This is going to be bad!*

"Your room looks like Ali Baba's cave, Rawan. I don't know how you can find anything in this mess."

"I promise, Mama, I'm going to clean up. I'm *starting* to clean, but . . . after I go to the bathroom . . ." She runs off.

Rawan spends most of that day in her room, folding and hanging the clothes that are scattered everywhere. There hasn't been time to do it lately, because of all the comings and goings—seeing Jad and Ghady and the kids in the neighborhood. Now, cleaning up helps her pass the time so she doesn't get bored. Rawan tries on her school uniform. The skirt needs to be just a little longer. She will have to take it to the tailor—she doesn't want to attract any unwanted comments on her first day back. She checks her books and notebooks and puts them in her bag. School is starting soon, and she wants to be sure she's ready. Seeing the uniform and books helps her digest the idea of going back to school—unthinkable only a few days ago—and now she can enjoy the rest of her break.

Rawan imagines her first day back: a different classroom, a new view from the window, a new teacher, and maybe new students . . . Some of the other kids say that the new material is really hard, and that she'll have to study a lot to get good grades. She also heard it might depend on the teacher: some are generous with grades, while others take students to task for the tiniest mistakes. Rawan hopes her teacher this year will be nice.

She misses her school friends so much!

Rawan imagines seeing her friend Noor, who spent the summer at her dad's in Dubai. She wants to hear what's new with Maya, who went with her mom and brothers to Saudi Arabia, where her dad works. Karen definitely spent her break in France. She is so lucky! She gets to go there every summer, because her mom has French citizenship. As usual, Raed spent time in the village, at his family home, which is surrounded by a beautiful garden. He barely comes to Beirut all summer, since he doesn't like going to the sea when it's hot. He likes to stay up in the mountains, visiting his relatives and playing with the other kids.

Rawan is thrilled to see a new e-mail from Ghady! She starts to write her answer before she even finishes reading it.

Thursday, September 4, 2008

Dear Ghady,

I feel the same in Beirut—it's been cold and empty since you left. I am so bored! Just imagine, yesterday I went to bed early for the first time in like two months . . . I'm trying to keep busy by organizing my room (which makes Mama happy) plus getting ready for school. I'm glad you're finally enjoying the peace and privacy of your room. The important thing is that you don't forget your friends . . . Jad called this morning, and he's missing you a lot. I'll tell him you said hi. We're going to meet soon at Uncle Fareed's and eat pistachio ice cream . . . mmm . . . mmmm . . . The poor Belgians are deprived of Uncle Fareed's ice cream . . . Ha ha ha ☺.

Wish you were here . . .

Best,
Rawan

ENCOUNTERS

GHADY HAS BEEN at Union School ever since his first year of elementary. It's a school for kids from all different countries who live with their families in Belgium, with classes taught in English. On his first day there, Ghady felt as if he were suffocating, and he's had the same feeling every first day since. When he was little, he would cry and tell his mom not to leave him—to bring him home with her. Now he's thirteen, and of course he doesn't cling to his mother any more. But the same feeling still pushes its way up.

When he gets to the playground, he looks around to find his best friend Daniel. It's chaos. So much noise. All the kids are caught up in the excitement of seeing each other. Then he spots Daniel waving to him. Ghady smiles and runs to meet his friend.

"Daniel!"

The boys hug, and their other friends show up around them: Matthias and Charlotte and Liza.

Everybody rushes to say hi and tell their news and hear stories about the summer vacation.

"You got so tan!" Charlotte tells Ghady.

"I spent a lot of time at the beach. And the summer sun in Lebanon is really scorching."

"You're lucky," Charlotte says. "I didn't go to the sea even once this summer. I stayed at my grandpa's house in northern France, and it rains all the time there. Ugh, it was so bad!"

Ghady and his friends swap a lot of news. Daniel talks about his trip to Ireland, where he met his mom's grandfather, who is 99 years old. Matthias tells them about Greece, and Liza about Rome.

The bell rings, interrupting their conversations.

"This is the worst part of school. Back to the classroom!" Matthias says.

They all laugh, and Liza says sarcastically that she's *jumping* for *joy*. "I mean, aren't you happy? We'll meet our eighth-grade teacher today. Yay."

Their laughter follows them into the classroom.

Like every year, Ghady picks a seat next to Daniel—they take two seats in the front row. The English teacher comes with a smile so wide it makes her tiny eyes almost completely disappear. "Welcome, everyone, to this new year. I am happy to see mostly familiar faces. I do notice three new students sitting in the back. You are welcome in our class . . . "

Ghady whispers to Daniel as he turns to look at the new kids: "And here's Ms. Laura, as usual, *so* eager to be back at work in the new year."

First period seems endless. The teacher explains their weekly schedule in great detail and tells them what they'll do in English class this year. Then, after Ms. Laura's period, the bell rings two more times before announcing the first break.

On the playground, Ghady sees one of the new students sitting on a bench, so he goes up to find out more about him.

"I'm Thomas," the new kid answers.

"Where were you last year?"

"I'm from Denmark. We moved here at the beginning of the summer because of my mom's work."

While Ghady and Thomas talk about life in Brussels and the school, Matthias and Daniel come up, curious about the new kid. Ghady feels that their interrogation is making Thomas nervous. They already got out of him that he has an older brother studying at a university in London, and that he lives with his mom. No dad in the house. Thomas doesn't say why. Ghady feels lucky that he, his parents, and his sister all live together in one house. About half the kids at his school have divorced parents, with the dad in one country and the mom in another. Ghady is always surprised when he hears that a kid has gone his whole life without ever having seen his dad. How could that be? You never heard about things like that in Lebanon. Plus, families there weren't just a mom, dad, brothers, and sisters, but also grandparents, aunts, uncles, and cousins.

Later that day, during the afternoon break, Ghady sits with Daniel in a corner of the playground, talking about different stuff. "I spent a lot of time with my cousin Jad at this one mall by the house, where they have all kinds of video games."

"Honestly? I didn't know you guys had malls and places where kids could go and play video games."

"Oh, Lebanon has everything. Beirut's just like any modern city. We also have the sea, and the mountains, and beautiful weather most of the yea—"

A voice behind Ghady interrupts him.

"You're lying! Your country is ugly and dirty. Plus, there are terrorists."

Ghady knows the voice before he turns to see its source. Michael. He's in ninth grade this year, and Ghady has known him ever since he first came to this school, seven years ago. He's used to Michael's insults. Any time Ghady is out enjoying himself on the playground, Michael will come and try to bother him. Today, Ghady decides to ignore the irritating comment and not let himself be provoked. He doesn't want to face Michael. Inevitably, it will lead to a fight, and the first day of school is not exactly the right time for a fistfight. Ghady ignores the comments, and he hears a loud, mocking laugh as Michael walks away. He also hears him yell: "Know what? You're a coward. Hahaha, you can't even defend yourself and your country. Hahaha!"

After Michael's comments, Ghady feels wound up. He tries to hide it, but Daniel can see he's upset. "Don't let him get to you," he says, trying to comfort Ghady. "He just wants to get under your skin."

"Don't worry about me," Ghady says. "Come on, let's shoot some hoops before the bell rings."

By the time Ghady gets home, he's exhausted. New teachers, a lot of classes, and classmates both old and new. Finally, he can take off his school clothes and relax.

That evening, Ghady makes sure his bag is ready for the next day. After dinner with his family, he washes up and gets ready for bed. He thinks about Rawan and Jad. A few days ago, he was with them, living a totally different life.

He finds the email from Rawan.

Tuesday, September 9, 2008

Dear Rawan,

Enjoy eating the ice cream . . . And have some pistachio for me. It's my favorite. ☺

Today was the first day of school in the new year. I was super happy to see Daniel—he's my good friend here, who I told you about. Eighth grade seems really hard. This year, we're going to study chemistry and physics. God help us!

Plus Rawan . . . there's something bugging me at school that I didn't tell you about before. Like I said, I'm the only Arab student. Some of the kids don't like me, and some of them even hate me, because my name is weird and my hair isn't blond and straight. Okay, to be specific, there's one kid, Michael, who really bothers me. My mom is always telling me to ignore him, but sometimes I just want to scream in his face. I mean, I want to tell him I love being an Arab and I love my country.

From now on, I'm not going to let him mock my name and how I look. I've been thinking about it a lot, and it makes me wish I could live with you guys in Lebanon.

But right now, let's forget him. I miss you guys. Tell me more about Jad, because calling him on the phone is so expensive. Do you guys still meet without me? Is he still spending his free time at the mall? Ha. I remember how mad my aunt was when we stayed there for hours and hours, spending all our money!

Rawan, I'm waiting for your news, so don't take forever to answer.

Yours,
Ghady

Ghady re-reads his email. Then he smiles and hits send.

TIME MACHINE

RAWAN POPS THE CD into her computer and starts listening to the songs that she recorded at the music store in town. She bops while softly singing the first song's lyrics, then, as she moves to the second, her voice climbs higher and higher. It feels good to be alive. She grabs her pencil case, brings it close to her mouth like a microphone, and starts belting out the words. For a few moments, it's her song, she's on stage, and her body sways along with the rhythm. *What a strange power music has over me! It carries us up, up, and above— into a completely different world.*

Rawan hears a light knock on her door. It opens, and Kumari–their housekeeper–pokes her head in. "Your mom, turn it down. She try sleep. Wow, song so good. I want copy, too. Pleaaase," she says in her broken Arabic.

"Okay, okay, I'll make a copy for you." Rawan smiles as she turns down the volume.

She decides to log into her email. A new message! Rawan lights up at Ghady's email. *Over there in Belgium, the school year starts early. Over here, we're lucky; we get a few extra vacation days before we start. Although honestly, what's the point? The school year is so hard and exhausting, and we never get a break. Even during the holidays, we have so much homework that you have to do it every day in order to finish, so it's not really a vacation, just school days in disguise.*

Although she's happy, Rawan is also worried about what she reads in Ghady's email. It's not the first time he's mentioned that he's the only   17

Arab in his entire school. He must be missing Lebanon as usual, and needing time to get over the distance. She sits at her desk and starts to type.

Thursday, September 11, 2008

My friend Ghady,
I was thrilled to read your email. You'll have to wait a few days before I can tell you about my first day back, because I'm still on vacation. ☺ I miss our outings and our endless chats. I hope this year flies by so it's summer again and we can hang out. I wonder when someone will actually invent a time machine—I mean, we've heard enough about it in movies and books. Everyone would definitely want one.

You know what I think? The kids who make fun of you are actually jealous. They're jealous of your good looks and your tanned skin. My friend Karen always tells me about how so many Europeans long for darker hair and skin. Supposedly they plan trips just so they can get that bronzed look. Think of it like that. Don't give them the time of day and ignore their comments, just like your mom says. Let them find out for themselves how funny and sweet you are.

Jad sends you a big hello. Imagine, he's totally ready to spend hours glued to his computer screen, but he finds it hard to write a two-minute email. He's busy getting ready for school and is spending ages in crowded bookstores to get his textbooks. I'm smarter than him, because I escaped the lines by buying my books at the start of the summer from a girl who just finished eighth grade. I bought them at half the price and the girl even gave me her notes and old tests!

That's all my news. As usual, I've rambled on a little . . . even though this is an email and not me talking aloud. I miss you.

Uncle Fareed sends you a special hello—he asked us about our curly-haired friend. ☺
Keep writing!

Your friend, Rawan

P.S. I don't enjoy pistachio ice cream as much as I used to. I wonder why.

GHADY SPEED-READS through a chapter they are supposed to discuss in class, then slips his book and notebook into his schoolbag.

"Finally done!" Ghady says to himself. "And now to the computer."

He checks his email. He smiles when Rawan's name pops up on the first message. Finally, she's replied. He's been waiting two days for her to answer. He skims through the lines. He flushes when he gets to the part where she says that he's good-looking. It makes him happy, and he hurries to answer, even though it's late and his parents think he's asleep.

Thursday, September 11, 2008

Rawan,

Your time machine idea is both clever and practical. We just have to invent it! For now, I guess email will do.

You guys are lucky. Hasn't school started yet? How is that fair? Why don't they give us a longer summer vacation?

Last time, I forgot to tell you that I'm starting to learn the oud. I have a lesson next week. My mom signed me up at the Arab Center for Arts and Culture in Brussels. She wanted to sign me up for Arabic lessons, too, but I said no. I still haven't changed my mind—it's so hard. I have a lot of classes this year, and I just won't have time to study Arabic. I know what you think. I remember the last day we spent in the tree house, when you tried to teach me to write my name in Arabic, so I could carve it into the tree next to yours and Jad's. Maybe next summer you can teach me how to write the letters and some simple words. Okay?

Ghady wants to write more, but he hears his dad's voice calling from the living room: "Ghady! Why is the light still on? Get to bed, please. No staying up on a school night."

"Okay, Dad."

He adds a last sentence, saying goodbye to his friend, then sends it with the sign-off:

Ghady, your friend forever

THE FIRST DAY

IT'S THE FIRST day of school. Rawan steps into the school-yard, eager to meet her friends. She hasn't seen them for the whole summer, and the only contact they had was a few emails. She turns to the right, then to the left, hoping to catch sight of one of them. She came early to find out which homeroom she'd be in, and which of her classmates would be with her. More importantly, she's excited to hear her friends' updates and the details of what went down over the summer.

She heads to the entrance of the building and straight to the bulletin board that has lists of homerooms with each student's name. She gets closer and starts reading:

Grade 8 Homerooms
Section A
Section B
Section C

Rawan keeps scrolling down the lists. It takes a while to find her name and the names of her friends. *How interesting.* Soon, she smiles as she reads aloud, "Maya, Noor, Raed, Rawan, Karen . . . yay!" She jumps for joy. *This year, we'll all be together again.*

A few minutes later, her friends start streaming into the schoolyard, one after the other. High-pitched squeals ensue, along with hugs and kisses as they all realize they are in the same homeroom.

Like at the start of every year, Noor puts her hand in her bag to pull out the new cellphone her dad bought her during her trip to Dubai. "Guys, look! It's from the newest mall in Dubai. The most expensive and latest model. It won't be available here for another few months—that's what they told us at the store." Then she adds proudly, "I'm probably the first person in Lebanon to own this phone. It has a lot of cool features that I'll tell you about later. I've got to hide it now before the principal catches me with it." She puts the phone back in her bag. "My dad also bought me clothes and tons of other stuff, all from the *best* shops. He loves me so much!"

That's Noor all right, Rawan thinks. *She'll never change. Obsessed with designer this, designer that.*

Maya tells them about the vacation she spent with her mom and brothers in Saudi Arabia. "Thankfully, Dad changed where we were staying this year and rented a house in a gated community. We had so much fun. There was a tennis court, a swimming pool, and a fitness club. What sucked is that most of the residents were on holiday, but we still had a blast with a Jordanian family and another Lebanese one we got to know. Every day, we'd wait for my dad to get back from work so we could explore places outside of the compound. Sometimes, we'd set off before noon in a private bus that took us to the souk and then brought us back at set times."

Karen, as always, rattles on about her awesome time in France, between Paris and the countryside. She talks about how beautiful the scenery is over there, how everything is so organized, and what a great time she had with her mom's French family. "You can't even imagine how good my cousins have it. Every Saturday, they stay out as late as they want with their friends. It's just the way they do things over there. Here, I've got to call a family meeting to get my dad's approval just to go to the movies or stay out till ten, *c'est impossible!* I mean, it's so tough being half French and half Lebanese."

Raed tells tales about adventures with his friends in the mountains—hunting trips and long bike rides. He talks about how he helped his mom cut grape leaves and prepare provisions for winter. His mom always insists on making everything by hand. She doesn't trust what they sell in the supermarkets these days.

Finally, it's Rawan's turn. She tells them about what she did over the summer with Jad and Ghady, the 'Belgian sweet,' as her friends nicknamed him. She tells them about their getaways to the mountains, their meetings in the walnut-tree house, and their grape and fig-picking competitions. She also talks about how they would ride their bikes, hang out in the neighborhood, and play volleyball in the sports club next to her house.

The bell rings for first period, cutting short the summer catch-up. Rawan and her friends shuffle to class, each with their own questions about the teachers and the subjects they would cover, each hoping this year would be easy, breezy, and fun.

GHADGHUD

GHADY'S CLASSES AND school projects keep him really busy. His two favorite days are Thursday and Friday, since those are the days he has his oud lessons, which he always eagerly awaits. He brought the oud over with him from Lebanon last year. His grandpa had bought it for him after Ghady said he wanted to learn to play. That day, Ghady had been surprised by the gift: "Grandpa, as soon as you know I want something, you get it for me right away."

"How many Ghadys do we have, *habibi*?" his grandpa had said.

His grandpa said that a lot, and it always made Ghady smile.

"Will you perform for us next summer, my Ghadghud?" his grandma had asked from behind her thick, black-rimmed reading glasses.

"*Teta*! Don't call me Ghadghud! I'm not a little kid anymore."

"Certainly, Mr. Ghady," she said, then sealed her lips with a sparkle in her eyes.

It's hard to play the oud, but Ghady practices every day—as soon as he's finished his homework, answered his messages, and chatted with his friends online. When his sister is in a good mood, she'll go into his room and ask about the songs he's working on. But when she's in a bad one, she'll turn on him and shout from her room, "Ahh, my poor ears! Ghady, stop that noise, I want to read!"

At times like those, Ghady wished he didn't have a sister to bother and boss him around whenever she liked. But when he really thought about it, he realized how lucky he was that Zeina listened to him and gave him advice. Lots of times, he took it. Besides, she was always willing to help him with math, and with the French he had to take as a second language. When he was four or five, Zeina—who was three years older—used to make him sit on a little chair, and she'd pretend to be the teacher. Back then, she gave him real lessons. She'd write letters and numbers with white chalk on a small board, and Ghady would copy it all down in his notebook. Between this and his grandpa, he learned to write English letters and to do simple math. By the time he started school, he was way ahead of the other kids. Zeina always entertained him with lots of stories about her friends and teachers, and he liked being with her when they went on vacation to different countries in Europe. Without her, he'd have to spend all his time with his mom and dad at museums and art exhibits. Nothing against museums or art, but sometimes he got bored when his mom insisted on visiting *every single one*. With Zeina there, he was allowed to leave the hotel without his parents, as long as they were back in time for lunch and hadn't bought too many souvenirs.

Ghady hasn't gotten an answer to his last letter to Rawan, which he sent more than a month ago. He opens his email, puts in her address, and writes:

Tuesday, October 28, 2008.

Hey Rawan!
Where are you? I've been thinking about you. I haven't gotten any messages from you over the last few weeks. Are you mad at me for something? Or maybe you're just busy with school and your school friends, and you forgot about me?
Write as soon as you get time, don't forget!

Ghady

BLURRED DAYS

FOR RAWAN, THE FIRST weeks of school fly by. She
doesn't notice time passing since she's so absorbed in her mountains of
homework. On the weekend, after she's finally finished, she remembers
that she hasn't checked her email in a while. She logs in and reads two
messages from Ghady. She decides to reply there and then.

Sunday, November 2, 2008

Dear Ghady,

Sorry for taking so long to get back to you. I'm not mad at you, I've just been
super busy lately with never-ending schoolwork that doesn't leave me any
free time to even check my email. Oh, Ghady! I miss the summer holidays so
much! Sleeping late, going out whenever we wanted . . .

I just read your two messages. Sure, our school starts later over here, but
the extra summer vacation is probably the only thing we've got going for us,
and you're jealous of that? Isn't it enough that in Belgium you have safety
and stability? At least you've got electricity 24/7. I so wish I could live abroad
and take advantage of what you have, instead of a few extra days of summer.
Think about how, over here, we're at the mercy of random electricity blackouts
and insane traffic. That's all on top of the daily back and forth between the
politicians. Two days ago, a fight broke out between two guys by my aunt's

house because of some comment about a politician's photo. The whole area was on lockdown because of it. Tell me, has that ever happened over there in Brussels?

I love that you're learning how to play the oud. That means next summer, you can play us some of your sweet tunes. Maybe playing a Middle Eastern instrument will give you the nudge you need to learn to read and write Arabic. Believe me, like I told you before, it's really not that hard. I mean, there are only twenty-eight letters. Kumari told me that in Sinhala, one of the Sri Lankan languages, there are fifty-two letters. Arabic is still easier than that! Think about it.

This year, I joined an art class in school. I'm going to try to seriously develop this childhood hobby of mine.

A week ago, I talked on the phone with Jad. He's busy studying. As usual, he finds every subject hard and needs a lot of time to do his HW. He's so stressed he didn't even tell me one of his jokes, like he usually does when we talk.

That's all I've got from my end.

The artist-to-be,
Rawan

P.S. Do your classmates know how funny and sweet you are? Tell me the latest. Are those kids still bullying you?

THOMAS

GHADY WAKES TO the sound of heavy rain. The sky is still dark, although the clock says it's seven. He hears his mom's footsteps approach his bedroom door. "Come on, Ghady. It's time for school."

"Rrghhh. I want more sleep." He yawns and stretches out on the bed.

Ghady drags himself to the bathroom to wash up, puts on his clothes, and goes down to the kitchen for breakfast. He finds his mom making cheese sandwiches for school, while Zeina is eating cornflakes with milk. Ghady takes out two slices of bread and slathers them with peanut butter and raspberry jam—his favorite breakfast. "Mom, I want to invite Thomas here on Friday after I'm back from my oud lesson. His mom says, if you say it's okay, he's allowed to sleep over."

"Thomas? That's a name I haven't heard before. Is he in your class?"

"Yeah," Ghady says. "He just started this year—he moved here from a school in Denmark. His mom's a translator with the EU."

"Okay, go ahead and invite him. You know I like to meet all your friends," his mom says. Then she urges him and his sister: "Come on, hurry up. We have to leave in five minutes if we're going to beat traffic."

Ghady's mom opens her big blue umbrella and walks out the front door, but Zeina doesn't walk under the umbrella as they run to the car, laughing. Ghady's foot slips and he falls down, soaking his jeans. They laugh even more.

"Oh, great. Look how you got your clothes dirty, Mister! I don't understand how you two prefer getting wet rather than just walking under the umbrella."

"I hate umbrellas—they were invented for adults!" Zeina says. "Walking in the rain is refreshing, Mama. Besides, our Eastpaks are waterproof, so our books won't get soaked."

Ghady laughs. "Actually, my hair looks cooler when it's wet."

"And are your pants also cool when they're wet?" his mom says.

Ghady doesn't answer, and Zeina laughs even harder. "Cool because they're sagging, and half his butt's hanging out."

Their laughter is long and loud.

Their mom suppresses her smile and drives off, muttering and pretending to look serious: "God help me! If one of you gets sick in this weather, then you'll have to stay home from school, which means I'll have to miss work."

"Calm down, Mama. We're not going to get sick. You take good care of us, and our bodies are strong as steel."

Zeina puts a hand on her mom's shoulder, and now her mom can't help but laugh at her mischievous daughter.

A DIFFICULT DAY

RAWAN DOESN'T HEAR HER phone alarm, even though she always wakes up before it goes off, then waits for it to ring while she lazes around in bed. Each morning, she savors a few minutes of laziness while watching the screen. She anticipates the moment it will flash the first time, then a second, before it blasts her favorite songs, which welcome the day with their robust beats.

After her mom hurriedly wakes her up, Rawan gets dressed. She scoops up her books and notebooks from the desk in the corner of her room, dumps them into her backpack, and dashes off to school.

She walks with quick steps, continually glancing at her watch, wishing the hour and minute hands would slow down a little and have mercy on her just this once, so she can reach school before the first bell rings. The distance between her house and the school seems endless, and it feels like she'll never make it. It gets worse when it starts pouring rain. *What great luck I have. The first time it's rained all year, and I'm also late and without an umbrella.* She knows today is going to be a rough one.

Rawan finally arrives at school, her hair and clothes soaked. She doesn't come across the principal on her way to class and breathes a sigh of relief. She enters to find that her friends have already started a math test. Wordlessly, the teacher hands her the test. Maybe she notices how worked up and anxious Rawan is, so she thinks better of saying anything, especially since this is the first time Rawan has ever been late. *Maybe because I'm soaking wet, she doesn't want to make it any worse. Thank you, rain.* When she reads the test, she doesn't understand a thing. She can't remember what she studied. It's as if the raindrops seeped into her head and washed away all the equations she had stayed up cramming late last night. Nothing changes for a few minutes, and Rawan feels an intense need to cry. But then, all of a sudden, her memory comes back to her, and what she thought was lost is now found. She tries to focus and solve the equation before her time runs out. She hands in her paper, her stomach knotted with tension. She's convinced that she forgot to write something down to show her work or made some kind of mistake because she went so fast and was so stressed out. She's pretty sure she won't get a good grade this time around.

Her other classes that day aren't any different. They are just as boring and just as long. When her Arabic teacher asks her to turn in her essay, she searches frantically in her backpack among her other papers but can't find it. She must have forgotten it on her desk in her room.

In the schoolyard, her friends' updates don't lighten her mood, even though some are pretty funny. Karen tells them she's decided to give up going to the movies if it means she doesn't have to eat any more peas and rice. Noor tries to coax Rawan into exchanging her old phone for a new one, so that what happened this morning won't happen again. Raed talks about how his mom prepared *qawarma* with eggs the day before, and he describes how delicious it was, to the point that everyone wants a taste and blames him for their sudden pangs of hunger.

DISILLUSIONED

AT SCHOOL, BECAUSE OF the rain, most of the kids stay under the sheltered part of the playground. There, overcrowding makes it hard to run or play sports.

Ghady finds Daniel in a corner reading a book and calls to him: "Daniel! This is break—it's time to relax, not read."

"But the book's so exciting," Daniel says without lifting his gaze. "I can't put it down."

Then Ghady hears Thomas calling. He turns to see him throwing a ball in the air, catching it, and tossing it up again.

"Come on, let's get out of here," Thomas says. "I can't stand the crowds on this tiny playground."

Ghady agrees, following him to the big playground—the one that has a volleyball net. They play in the rain for a while before Ghady sees that Michael and his friends are walking up to them. Ghady goes up to Thomas and whispers in his ear: "We don't want them to hang around with us. That's Michael, and I seriously cannot stand how stupid he can be. Plus, he's with Larry, Sam, and Andy. They're even worse."

"I know Michael," Thomas says, in a voice that seems to be deliberately loud, just to irritate Ghady. "He's my friend, too, and this is his ball. I borrowed it from him this morning."

"I'm going to play with them," Thomas adds.

Ghady goes back to the covered part of the playground, his hair and clothes soaked. He sits in the corner by Daniel.

Daniel closes his book. "What's going on? You look mad."

"Nothing," Ghady says. "It's not important."

"Did you have a fight with Thomas?"

"No, but listen to this: He's friends with those guys—Michael and his gang of friends. Can you believe it?"

"Why let it bother you?"

"Because Michael's racist. And Larry and Sam and Andy follow him without thinking, doing whatever he says. Sheep!"

Daniel laughs. "I think you're exaggerating a little. Let's go to class. The bell's going to ring in a couple of seconds."

The idea of Thomas being friends with Michael's group needles Ghady, but he'll let it go this time.

Friday, on his way back from the Arab Center for Arts and Culture, Ghady goes with his mom to get Thomas for the sleepover, just like they'd planned. At the house, the two boys spend most of their time playing Guitar Hero on the Playstation in Ghady's room, and they don't stop until they're super hungry. Then they go to the kitchen. They find dinner already on the table: spaghetti bolognaise.

"Yum! The food looks delicious, Mom."

"Come sit. I'll call Zeina and tell her to join you for dinner."

"And you?" Ghady asks. "Aren't you hungry?"

"I'm waiting for your dad. He'll be here in a little bit."

Thomas and Ghady stay up until around midnight. They talk in the dark after they've laid down to sleep—Ghady on his bed, and Thomas on a mattress Ghady's mom set out on the floor. They talk about school, the teachers, the other kids. Ghady thinks this is the right time to ask Thomas: "What do you like about Michael and those guys? They're so irritating, and they pick on other kids for no reason."

"Michael?" Thomas says. "It's the opposite—he was the first one to come up to me when I got to the school, and we became friends right away. I always go over to his house."

Ghady feels a wave of disappointment.

"Yeah, it's true, I forgot. You're Danish."

"What's that supposed to mean?" Thomas asks.

Ghady doesn't want to talk about it anymore. Thomas isn't going to understand about Michael's racism tonight. "It's not important. We're pretty much asleep. Good night." To end the conversation, he changes his position, moving his head on the pillow and picking up the blanket 33 that fell to the ground and pulling it over himself. Not even a minute passes before Ghady can tell Thomas has fallen asleep. But he can't drop off. He's thinking about Rawan. He still hasn't answered her last message. How could he have forgotten? He gets up from his bed and walks to the computer.

Friday, November 13, 2008

My friend,

Do you ever feel really tired but you can't fall asleep? That's what it's like for me tonight. On the subject of power cuts, like you were saying, for me they're not a big deal. It's the opposite—I love candlelight at night instead of a light bulb. Do you remember when you and your parents came to my grandpa's house for dinner? That day, the power was cut, and the building's generator was out of gas. So we ate by candlelight. It was really nice.

I'm glad you're studying drawing. Lately, my mom's been busy turning the small glass room that overlooks our garden into her new art studio. Right now, it's filled with all these small oil paintings.

She'll be happy when I tell her you're an artist, too. ☺

Ghady

STRANGE FEELINGS

RAWAN CAN'T BELIEVE this school day has finally ended. She goes back home feeling worn out—shattered, actually—as if she has climbed a mountain. She enters the kitchen to find her mom making lunch. She kisses her. "What's for lunch today, Mom?

"Peas and rice. I haven't made this dish for ages. Come on, the food's ready. Your dad and brother will join us shortly." *What a weird coincidence. I don't like peas and rice either, and Mom only thought to make it today of all days?*

Rawan isn't the only one who feels uneasy. At lunch, she picks up on her dad's unusual silence. He doesn't joke around with her or ask what's new, and he even snaps at Rani when he asks for money to go out with his friends that evening. Rani's nineteen, and he started college this year, which means more freedom, going out with his friends, and of course, extra pocket money. Rawan is surprised. It's the first time her dad has ever refused Rani money: he's the spoiled one who gets whatever he wants without ever having to lift a finger.

After going to her room to be alone, Rawan checks her email and finds one from Ghady. Her lips curve up into a small smile, maybe for the first time today. "Finally you answer, Brussels sprouts," she says aloud as she responds to his email right away.

November 14, 2008

Hey Ghady,

I totally get you. I was also so sleepy, but to the point that I didn't wake up. That's what happened to me this morning. On top of that, I was forced to walk to school in the rain, got soaked, was late to class and my math test, forgot my Arabic essay at home . . . in addition to a series of other unfortunate events that 'spiced up' my day.

Basically, it was a tough day ☹, and now I feel like I'm coming down with a cold. As for the blackouts, Monsieur Romance, try to put yourself in my shoes. Like today, I was forced to take the stairs to my apartment, with my backpack, after everything that happened. I climbed 105 steps!!

All my news isn't bad, though. I'm having fun with my friends in school, and I really am loving my art class. We've started with pencil drawings. We're supposed to learn how to use color soon, which I'm dying to master.

Soon, it's going to be class representative election time. I plan on running, and I've been thinking about a platform I can share with my class. What do you think? Any suggestions for what to include?

Now I've got to go, not to bed, but to eat. I'm starving, which means I must be feeling a little better. I'm going to make an apricot jelly and butter sandwich. Yum, yum. ☺

From,
Hungry Rawan.

SCHOOL BULLIES

THE MUSIC TEACHER, Ms. Lilian, asked each kid to choose a musical instrument, research it, and present about it in class. Ghady decided to talk about his favorite: the oud. The day of the presentation, he comes to school carrying his oud in its black case. When his friends spot him on the playground, they gather around. Charlotte and Liza ask him to take it out and show them. At first, Ghady refuses. But faced by the two girls' insistence, he soon gives in. The oud comes out of the bag, and Ghady flushes with pride, feeling himself at the center of everyone's attention. "What's that?" asks Susanna, a girl in his class.

"It's called an *oud*," Ghady says. "In my research, I found that in Arabic, *oud* means wood."

"Oouuuood . . . ouuudd . . . I can't pronounce it," Susanna says, laughing. "Can I touch the strings?"

"How many are there?" asks another kid, Elián. "Six? Like a guitar?"

"Nope, there are eleven," Ghady explains. "A long time ago, they were made from animals' intestines."

"That's disgusting!" Susanna says, taking two steps back. "I'm not coming any closer. Those strings definitely stink."

Everyone laughs.

"Come on, Susanna. Are you kidding? Nowadays, the strings are made of nylon."

"Play us something," Daniel says.

"Nah. After music class with Ms. Lilian." Ghady puts the oud back in its black case.

In class, he talks for more than ten minutes about the oud. He feels lucky that the other kids are interested in its long history, which goes back more than five thousand years, to the times when it was played in the palaces of long-ago kings. When he's done speaking, Ms. Lilian asks him to play a little.

Ghady sits on the teacher's chair, adjusts the oud's strings, and starts to play the song "She's Leaving Her Father's House." This is his favorite, although he still hasn't been able to memorize the words in Arabic, even though his mom plays the CD over and over. Everyone listens attentively, and Charlotte and Liza even cheer.

The teacher praises Ghady for his excellent research and beautiful playing, especially since he only started his lessons a couple of months ago.

At the afternoon break, kids gather around him, including Matthias, Daniel, and Thomas, while he plays them some Arab melodies.

"What, do you think you're a musician or something? What's *that* thing you're playing? It looks hideous, and the sound is horrific."

It's Michael's voice, and he walks up with a steady confidence, his chest puffed out like he's ready to start a fight. He turns to the boys in his group, gesturing for them to back him up.

"Ha ha ha." Larry and Andy laugh, and each of them says something worse than the last. Then Ghady stops. "Okay, enough! What makes you guys think you're so special? You just don't get anything."

Michael steps up, his hand shooting out, trying to grab the oud from Ghady's hands. Without thinking, Ghady resists. Deep inside, he's been expecting this kind of underhanded move, and now he holds onto the oud with all his strength. But Michael's grip is stronger, and he yanks it out of Ghady's arms.

Michael laughs. "I can break it if I want."

"No!" Ghady shouts. Then someone is tapping his shoulder. It's Thomas.

"Come on, Michael. Give Ghady his oud back. Why are you doing this?"

Michael doesn't answer. He stands in place for a few seconds, staring sharply into Ghady's eyes. Then he steps back. He talks briefly with his group before he turns and flings the oud at Ghady.

Ghady's heart seizes up. He's terrified the oud will hit the ground, but he catches it at the last moment, and it doesn't fall, doesn't break. Ghady heaves a sigh, his blood still boiling. He wants to lift up his oud and smash it down on Michael's head. He wants to scream in Michael's ears until he goes deaf. He wants to kick Michael until he falls to the ground. But he doesn't do any of those things. He just watches Michael walk away with the other boys, their laughter ringing in his ears.

Ghady's anger quickly cools, and now he can feel tears on his face. His friends Daniel, Charlotte, Matthias, and Liza circle around him. He doesn't see Thomas, and he wonders where he's gone.

"Don't think about them anymore," Matthias says. "Nobody in school can stand them. And some day, they're going to pay for this."

Ghady returns the oud to its case, trying to hold back tears. Daniel puts an arm around him. "They're cowards. And when they do stuff like this, it just makes people hate them even more. Yesterday, I saw Larry and Andy take a kid's coat and toss it around on the playground. The poor kid was crying and following them, and they were *laughing*. I don't understand why they do stuff like that."

"I think they just want attention," Liza says. "They want us to think they're strong and everybody else is weak."

"Maybe." Charlotte pushes Ghady's long curly hair off his eyes to see if he's still crying.

"Come on," Daniel says. "Let's go have some lunch before the break's over."

They all stand up, and Ghady wipes his nose with the edge of his coat and squeezes his eyes to get the tears out. Then they head for the cafeteria.

That evening, Ghady tells his mom and dad what happened, and about how Michael is always harassing him.

"You want us to call his mother?" his mom asks.

"Please, no. That just gives him more of a reason to call me a coward."

"Then don't be afraid of him," his dad says. "Face him, and, if he tries to hurt you, go straight to the principal."

"Okay, sure," Ghady says.

When the phone rings, Zeina is helping Ghady with his math homework. It's a call for Ghady—from Thomas. They talk for almost an hour, and Ghady hangs up only after several complaints from his dad, who is standing in front of him with his arms folded, waiting for an important work call.

"What's so important that it couldn't wait for tomorrow?" his dad asks after Ghady hangs up.

"Nothing special. It was just a friend, and we were talking about school and friend stuff."

Ghady lies down on his bed, thinking about the conversation. The whole long talk was Thomas trying to get him to reconsider his relationship with Michael—to be friends with him. But Ghady's answer was absolute: He doesn't want to be one of Michael's "followers." Who does he think he is?

Ghady jumps out of bed, as if to shake off Michael's whole annoying story. He sits in his desk chair and opens his email. There, he finds a message from Daniel, plus one more. He smiles. The second one is from Rawan.

He reads Daniel's message first.

Thursday, November 19, 2008

Don't worry about Michael. Everyone knows he's a jerk, plus he's a fourth-class student and a first-class idiot. See you tomorrow.

Daniel

After that, he reads the letter from Rawan. But he's exhausted and doesn't know what to say to her. He doesn't want to bother her with everything going on in his life, so he answers in a few words.

Thursday, November 19, 2008

Hi Rawan,

I'm so happy to get your letter. Sorry I can't write much today, I'm really exhausted.

Love,

Ghady

Ghady tries to sleep, but it's hard—he can never sleep after he gets into a fight with Michael. He turns the computer back on. Without switching on his room light, he goes over to write Rawan again.

Thursday, November 19, 2008

Hi again,

Okay, I really need to tell you about some things that are happening because of that kid Michael. I can't stand him. But I don't want to talk about that now—another time. If you knew how much I miss you and Lebanon!! There, I feel like everyone gets me, plus there aren't any boys flexing their muscles and bullying people. Uggh, some people are so irritating! Okay, let's forget them now, otherwise I'll have nightmares when I sleep tonight—if I fall asleep. ☹

Did I tell you that I've gotten really good at the oud, and that I can play a lot of Arab songs now? I've learned five really well, and I'm working on more. I'm definitely bringing the oud this summer so you can hear me play. Ohhkay. I have to go to bed and try to sleep.

Until the next email.

Ghady

CAMPAIGN PREP

EVEN THOUGH HER MOM tells her more than once to go to bed, Rawan stays up late, absorbed in making posters and writing slogans for her election campaign. She prepares the agenda she'll share with her classmates, and which will be the deciding factor in whether or not she's elected class representative this year. Rawan is giddy. She never thought about running for the position before. It was always enough for her to support whichever of her friends ran, especially by designing posters and coming up with slogans. After all, her friends call her "The Queen of Creativity," since her clever drawings speak for themselves.

Rawan thinks about the unusual competition that has grown between her and Noor, who is also running for the same post. Their friends will have to choose between the two of them. Fun, but awkward at the same time. Rawan smiles when she remembers Noor's words, "Now we'll see who's more popular, Rawan! Won't that really be something."

Rawan flings her head back against her soft pillow and sinks into it. She is so tired! She didn't think a small election campaign like this would take so much effort. It's taking up more time than studying for a math or science test. She hasn't asked her friends to help, because she doesn't want them to feel awkward in front of Noor . . . This way, it will be fair and square.

The next day, Rawan has to force herself awake. She hears her musical alarm, but it's so hard to drag her body out of bed. She feels like a tree whose roots are set deep into the ground, refusing to be uprooted. She tries to sit up, but her body won't obey. She's beyond exhausted, even though today hasn't even begun.

"Rawan! Get up now, you're late. I knew this was going to happen. You were up late wasting time drawing and . . . " Her mom's voice sails through to break the chains that had bound Rawan to bed. She's able to charge her body with just enough energy to get free.

Rawan shuffles into the kitchen to drink a glass of chocolate milk and eat her morning banana. She finds her mom and brother there. "Mama, I wasn't wasting time. I was preparing for my election campaign. Today we have to share our plans for the year with the whole grade. It's really important to me, so you should be encouraging me and supporting me!"

Her mother comes up and kisses her cheek. "You're right, sweetheart. I'm sorry. Best of luck. You deserve to win, and of course I support you."

"My sister is in the running. Oh man! And Mom is backing her. I'll back you, too, Rawan. I have an idea." He laughs. "I'll plaster your photo on all the walls around the neighborhood!"

"Stop making fun of me! I don't need *that* kind of help, Rani. Your support is enough to bring me down."

"Is the job really worth all this work? What will you get out of it? You're acting like you're running for a municipal or parliamentary seat!" he shoots back.

"Yes, it's worth it. It means a lot to me, just like making the college basketball team means a lot to you. Remember how depressed you were when they didn't pick you the first time? Didn't you stay holed up in your room for two days while everyone was trying to cheer you up?" she asks, making her way to her room.

While she gets dressed, Rawan reflects on what she said to her brother. *Maybe I laid it on too thick, but he's the one who's always looking for a fight.* She is surprised that her mom didn't intervene. She usually has her line about how siblings should get along and treat each other kindly.

In class, the students give a warm welcome to the agendas presented by the candidates for class representative. The suggestions for improvement, and the projects they promise to do during the year, are all pretty similar: more class trips; less homework, especially during vacation; more types of food in the cafeteria, including healthy options, like a Lebanese breakfast spread; having a costume ball; and other ideas.

Rawan's classmates really like her drawings and the original comments she prepared. They also ooh and aah at Noor's designs, which she got online, adding slogans in colored letters before she printed them off. The teacher asks the students to think long and hard before they choose a candidate, announcing that the time of the vote will be decided soon.

On the playground, when the friends get together under the giant oak tree, Rawan tells Raed about her late night drawing her posters. Noor says, laughing, "Poor you. I finished everything on the computer by one in the afternoon, and then I went to the souk with my mom. I came home, watched TV, and slept like a baby. It's true that you're the 'Queen of Creativity,' but I'm the 'Mother of Quick Thinking.'"

"Actually, Rawan's drawings are really beautiful, Noor," Raed says. "Are you comparing beautiful, handcrafted art with a machine?"

"Who else, other than *you*, Raed, appreciates handmade stuff?" She distances herself, then goes on. "Handmade tomato paste, blossom water, apricot jam, *za'tar*, *qawarma* . . . " Everyone laughs, and even Raed—who is red-faced at the beginning—bursts out laughing.

Rawan goes home thinking of Jad, who she decides to call "summer friend" from now on, because she only sees him in the summer. He's in another school, busy with classes, and he goes out with his school friends whenever he gets the chance. She decides to call him that evening. First, she'll scold him, and then she'll get his news. Rawan is surprised to find her dad at home—he usually gets home after her.

"Baba! You're home early. That's great, because I'm starving. Mom, is the food ready? Can we eat now?"

Today, Rawan also notices that her dad isn't himself. He smiles at her, but he doesn't give her his famous bear hug. Her mom is also acting strange. She doesn't ask Rawan about school or grades or even about what she presented to the class today. Rawan waits for her mom to ask even one question about the elections, so that she can tell her everything, "from A to Z," as Ghady says. But she doesn't ask. Her mom dishes out the food, distracted to the point that she spills some broth on the beloved colorful tablecloth she always frets over. She doesn't rush to clean it, but instead keeps on as if nothing has happened. Rawan feels more troubled than before. For a few days now, she's picked up on a change in how her parents are acting. Her father is tightlipped, not joking with anyone, and her mother has become short-tempered, also barely speaking. *I wonder why?*

While they're eating lunch, Rawan asks her dad, "Baba, why did you come home early today?" It's the only question she can think of to get her dad to speak. His answer is curt. "I've taken a long holiday from work. I want to rest a bit."

"Then we can go out every day after school's out! You can take us anywhere, right?" Rawan says, psyching herself up to change the stilted atmosphere. But her dad answers in a decisive tone, without even looking at her. "I said I want to rest."

Why isn't Baba happy? Usually people are happy when they're on vacation, but he doesn't look happy from any angle.

Rawan enters her room confused. There, she comes up with reasons for the change in her parents' behavior, especially her dad. She'll ask her mom about it next time she gets the chance.

She opens her email and reads Ghady's message. She decides to write him a quick response.

Tuesday, November 25, 2008

Dear Ghady (or would you prefer that I call you The Oud King?),

I miss you, too. I thought of you last night when I was making the posters for my election campaign. I imagined what you'd say about the slogans I wrote to convince my friends to choose me. "Rawan's your rep . . . Choose Rawan now . . . " You didn't give me your suggestions, Monsieur. ☹

I'm really dying to hear you play the oud! It looks like we're going to have some great summer nights with the sweet songs you'll be playing us.

Ghady, as for that boy Michael, maybe it's better for you to totally ignore him. And whenever you feel annoyed by him, practice your oud. This is my "Rawan for your success" advice. You'll see — this way, you'll learn a lot of songs fast. ☺

Lazy Jad never calls. It's like he's forgotten all about me. ☹ That saying, 'Out of sight, out of mind' really was made for him. Don't get mad at him. I'll talk to him today and give him a piece of my mind, then I'll invite him to have a fruit parfait with honey, cream, and nuts at Uncle Fareed's.

I wish you could come with us.

Love,
Rawan

Rawan is worn out. She didn't sleep the night before. She decides to lie down for a bit. That way, maybe her energy will come back, and she can then finish her homework before she calls Jad. As soon as her head hits the pillow, she falls into a deep sleep.

BEHIND THE GYM

ON THE PLAYGROUND, snow has been falling since the night before, and Ghady and his friends are gathering clumps of it, making them into big balls, and hurling them. They laugh. They run. They yelp when they see snowballs heading straight for them. The loudest screams come from Liza, Charlotte, Elián, and Susanna, especially when the snow slides down under their clothes. In the middle of this snow battle, Thomas comes up and takes Ghady aside. Ghady gives him a questioning look, but Thomas offers no explanation until they've moved away from the group.

"Come with me. But don't let Daniel or Matthias or Charlotte or Liza see you."

"What's over there?"

"It's something fun, and you'll thank me for it. Come on. Hurry up, and don't ask too many questions."

Thomas tugs on Ghady's arm, and Ghady smiles, even though he's feeling a little nervous.

They go behind the gym, which is the building farthest from the playground and from the eyes of the supervisors. There, they find Michael and his group, smoking.

Ghady turns to Thomas. "Why did you bring me here? You know I don't smoke."

"This isn't a regular cigarette, stupid, it's a lot better than that. You have to try it."

As Thomas speaks, Michael stands up and walks over to Ghady. "You seriously don't know how to relax and enjoy yourself. Just take it. Take the joint and tell me what you think."

Ghady is surprised by Michael's tone—he's talking softly, and his face looks as though he's about to laugh.

"No thanks. I don't want it," Ghady says, in a hurry to get away.

Thomas grabs his coat to stop him from leaving.

"Let go of me, Thomas!"

"Not before you try this. Seriously, you are not going to regret it. You'll like it so much you'll ask for more. You'll see!"

"I told you to let me go," Ghady shouts, wrenching himself out of Thomas's grip.

"Jeez, I didn't mean to make you mad, Ghady. Why can't you just take things easy?"

Ghady yells as he backs away: "I don't understand you! First you defend me when he's bugging me, and now you drag me right to him. What's your problem?"

"You're the one making problems!" Thomas answers in a tone sharper than Ghady expected.

Ghady doesn't answer. Instead, he quickly walks away without waiting for Thomas, who follows him.

Ghady thinks a lot about this encounter, and about everything going on around him. Why did Thomas drag him to those boys? Why him?

He's been invited to Thomas's on Friday, and his dad already agreed to it. After all, his dad met Thomas and his mom, who came to pick him up the day he slept over. Should he go?

"If you like spending time with him, why not?" Zeina says, when he goes into her room that night to ask her opinion.

"I don't want to lose him as a friend," Ghady says. "But I don't get what he likes about Michael or why he believes him."

"You're smart, you can figure it out. In any case, don't let Michael wreck your friendship with Thomas."

The next morning, when he meets Thomas on the playground, Ghady smiles, trying to ease the tension that's come between them. Thomas slings his left arm around Ghady's shoulder. "You still mad about yesterday?"

Ghady says nothing, and Thomas goes on, whispering: "I want you to be a man, be brave, hang out with the kids who've got the power . . . That's all it is."

Ghady gives a half-smile, unconvinced. They walk together into the classroom, and the day passes without any problems.

That night, when Ghady reads Rawan's letter, he's gripped by a sudden sadness. He writes:

Thursday, November 27, 2008

My friend,

I want so badly to be in your school instead of mine! We could work on your campaign, do our homework together sometimes, and we'd do cool stuff on the weekends with Jad.

I mean, don't worry too much about me—I like my friends here, and I have fun being with them. But honestly, sometimes I feel like a stranger here. Even Thomas, who's my good friend this year . . . Well, I'm starting to get suspicious of our friendship. But I'm going to take your advice and put all my anger into the music. And you, Miss—you'll have to start a new painting just for me. I want to put it up in my room. ☺

Best,
Ghady

STRANGE SITUATION

RAWAN WAKES UP to the noise of an intense fight. She opens her eyes and looks around, disoriented. *Maybe it's coming from outside the house.* She listens closely and is shocked when she recognizes the voices: her parents.

She can't believe this is happening. Maybe it's a nightmare? No, she's not dreaming. She's awake in her room, and she knows these voices. This is the first time she's ever heard her parents exchanging these kinds of words. Thoughts start swirling around in her head, and she remembers how weird they've been acting lately. She tries to pinpoint when it started, but she can't remember. She tries to rewind her memory, day by day, but it's no use. Maybe it started a long time ago, and she didn't notice because she was always so caught up in her classes or friends or with the TV or computer.

The voices go quiet, and Rawan comes out of her room to find her father in the living room, sullen, puffing a cigarette in front of the TV. Her mom is sitting in her bedroom, teary-eyed. Kumari stands at the kitchen door, watching from afar, worry written all over her face. Rawan is confused. What should she do? Should she go over to her dad and speak with him, or hug her mom and comfort her? She decides to go back to her room and stay there. She sits at her desk and opens a book, but her gaze remains fixed on one word for a very long time. She doesn't feel like studying or chatting with Jad, even though it might calm her down. She puts her head, heavy with disturbing thoughts, down on her pillow once more, and she sleeps until the next morning.

Rawan doesn't know how many days pass like this—they're all the same. Her dad is at home, and the cigarette never leaves his hand. He barely speaks to her mom, and sometimes he leaves the house and doesn't come back until very late. Her mother is irritable. She seems sad and preoccupied all at once.

Eating lunch or dinner with the family isn't fun, like it used to be. There's no conversation or jokes, just the clinking of spoons, knives, and forks as they scratch against the plates. Sometimes, her mom asks routine questions, such as, "How was your day, Rawan? How was your day, Rani? What's new at school?" Rani and Rawan always answer these questions with their own stock reply, "Good." Rawan starts to hate coming home. She finds the walls cold, her room boring, and the atmosphere always tense. She no longer finds peace and safety in it. Even Rani the pampered one starts getting his fair share of scolding. Whenever he asks for the money he's been used to getting at the snap of his fingers, he is peppered with questions from their dad, "What did you do with the money you took yesterday? When will you stop asking? Maybe you should take an interest in your studies instead of going out and spending money on ridiculous things or wasting all your waking hours on the phone."

Rawan tries to pump Kumari for information about her parents' fight, and she replies, " Don't know. Mama always sad. Baba always sad. And me too, sad."

Rawan stops caring about her progress in school. What's the point if no one else cares? Whenever she opens her textbooks or notebooks to study, she finds herself mindlessly drawing circles and lines on the corners of the pages, sometimes for hours.

One night, before she gives in to sleep, she opens her email to find Ghady's latest message. She reads it, but without her usual grin. Ghady's emails make her happy, but this time her fierce concern for her parents weighs her down to the point where she can't smile anymore.

Thursday, December 1, 2008

Dear Ghady,

I also wish that you could be in my school. I have a lot of friends at school, but, at a time like this, I only want to talk to you. I need to share what's going on in my head with someone who understands me and can make me feel better. ☹

I'm trying to focus on drawing these days, because it relaxes me, like music does for you. I'll have to think about what to draw for you.

How are things at school? Do you still feel like you stick out? I won't take up any more of your time because I'm tired today.

Love,
Rawan

MADNESS

WHEN GHADY GOES OVER to Thomas's, things are normal at first: they talk, they play, they eat, they watch TV . . . But then Thomas's mom leaves to have dinner with her friend. Ghady didn't expect that. The boys are alone in the apartment.

When Ghady is immersed in a war game on the Playstation, he catches a strange smell drifting in from the balcony off Thomas's room. He lifts his eyes to see Thomas gesturing for him to come over.

Ghady steps out onto the balcony. "What are you doing, crazy? Is this the same thing Michael was smoking at school?"

"Ha! Yeah. I bought some joints from him. Want to try it?"

"N . . . No."

"Why? Just one time's not going to hurt you."

"You're crazy. What if you get addicted?"

"Don't be ridiculous. One joint is not going to affect you. Take it. Try it. You're not even going to feel anything."

Ghady hesitates. He feels sure this is a mistake. He remembers something about drugs his mom told him last year—about her friend Mariam's son. He died while doing drugs. Back then, she told him and Zeina: "Poor Mariam. Her son was eighteen, and she just couldn't help him shake his addiction. Some jerks in the neighborhood got him into drugs, and he died of an overdose one night, when he was over at a friend's." This story left a mark on Ghady, especially because he knew his mom's friend. She used to visit them a lot during their summers in Lebanon.

He isn't about to tell Thomas this story, since Thomas would make fun of him, and he doesn't want to be called a coward again. How can he prove to Thomas that he's brave and daring and not some perfect angel?

Why not try it? Just once.

Slowly and hesitantly, Ghady takes the joint from Thomas's hand. He takes a drag, but then he doesn't know how to get the smoke out of his lungs, so he ends up having a coughing fit. Thomas laughs. Ghady laughs.

"What was that?" Ghady says hoarsely. "Seriously, how do you do that so the smoke doesn't suffocate you?"

"Wait. Like this." Thomas slows down his movements so Ghady can follow. "Come on," Thomas says. "Try it again."

Ghady tries it. Once. Twice. Three times. Now, he doesn't cough as he exhales. When he finishes the joint, his head is spinning. He goes back into the room and sits in Thomas's desk chair.

"My mom will be here soon," Ghady says. He tries to stand, but his body is too heavy. "I'm going to go wash my face, and I'm never doing that again. You're crazy."

In the car, Ghady gives short answers to all his mom's questions.

"Did you have fun?"

"Yeah."

"What did you do?"

"Played."

"What did you eat?"

"Pizza."

When they get home, Ghady goes straight to his room and shuts the door. He looks into the mirror and sees two reddish eyes, puffy with exhaustion . . . He feels guilty and nervous. Is he just drowsy, or is there something else? He feels scared, too. Is this how addicts get started? They have a first experience, then a second, then a third? He whispers to himself: "Nah. I just did it out of curiosity and that's it. It's not going to happen again. I won't do it after today."

Ghady turns on his computer, hoping to find a message from Rawan. Two words from her would make him feel so much better.

He reads, then answers.

Friday December 5, 2008

Rawan,

I guess things aren't going so well—your letter was so much shorter and more serious than normal. What's up? I don't think it was short just because you were tired, like you said. Seriously, what is going on? What's bothering you? Is it someone at school?

I'm upset, too, and I was hoping a letter from you would change my mood, but now I'm worried about you. Don't forget that we're friends, Rawan, and that we can share everything with each other.

I'll start with me. Okay, I did something stupid tonight. At Thomas's, I agreed to smoke a joint. I'm such a moron! Don't worry, it's the first and last time. I hope you don't hate me because of it.

Your friend who's stupid sometimes,
Ghady

THE PHONE CALL

A FEW DAYS before the election for class representative, Rawan is sitting idly in class. She looks out the window. She stares at the heavy raindrops that splatter against the window pane, then stream down in rivulets, each a small waterfall. She doesn't take in a word of what her teacher is saying. She can't stop thinking about what's happening at home.

Her English teacher asks her to read aloud from the homework assignment that's due. Rawan doesn't respond. She keeps staring at the water streaming down the window pane. Her teacher calls out to her in a louder voice, which causes Rawan to start, as if she's waking up from a dream. The teacher repeats her instructions, more forcefully this time. Rawan opens her notebook, squints at the white lines, then says softly, "I didn't do it." The teacher is taken aback by her admission. She noticed Rawan has been falling behind the past few days and not completing assignments. "I want to talk to you at break please," she says.

After hearing what her teacher has to say, Rawan leaves to meet her friends by the gym, in the corner of the canopied schoolyard. This is where they get together when it rains.

"What happened?" Maya asks. "What did she say to you?"

"Nothing. She asked me why I hadn't done my homework, and I told her I was sick."

"And were you really sick?" Noor asks.

Rawan answers, not making eye contact with her friends, "Kind of. I mean, I was really tired."

A heavy sadness fills Rawan's eyes, and her friends notice. Soon enough, the sadness morphs into small, embarrassed, hot tears rolling down her cheeks. She tries to stop them but can't. Karen puts a hand on Rawan's shoulder and asks, concerned, "Are you okay? What's wrong?"

At this, Rawan starts sobbing—she can no longer hold back the storm inside. Her friends crowd around her, asking what's happening and why she's been someone else lately. They urge her to tell them, reassuring her that her secret will go no further than their circle. Rawan finally agrees and tells them about the change in her parents' behavior, and about the stressful environment at home that's tying her stomach up in knots. She's afraid that their fighting means they are going to separate. Noor comes up to Rawan and laughs. "Is that all? If they're always fighting and can't see eye to eye, then it's so much better if they get a divorce. My parents are divorced and look at me, am I complaining? I have the best of both worlds. My mom is in Lebanon and my dad is in Dubai. Mom spoils me and does whatever I ask, and Dad does the same when I visit him over there. They buy me anything and everything I want from the most expensive designers. Each wants me to love them more than the other, which means that I'm the one who comes out the winner."

"But I don't want them to get divorced. I want them to stay together, so that I can love them together!" Rawan shouts.

"Maybe it's just something really small, and you're making yourself sick with worry by blowing it up. Ask your mom, and she'll tell you what's going on. Instead of guessing and being scared, attack the problem head-on. Tell your parents how you feel. It's your right to know. You're not a kid anymore."

Raed adds, "If you share how you're feeling, maybe they'll be more conscious of how they're acting. So you'll actually be helping them out. My mom always says that families underestimate what kids can do, age is just a number."

Maya scoffs. "And when exactly does your mom tell you this? When she's asking you to cut grape leaves or pluck olives?" Maya's quip lightens Rawan's mood, and she bursts out in giggles at the sight of Raed chasing Maya to exact revenge for her snarky comment.

When Rawan gets home, she comes to a decision. What's been bothering her for the past few days will come to an end, and she'll no longer have to carry this burden—but she has to get Rani's two cents first. It's better to hear what he thinks, even though she's pretty sure   57 that he's clueless about what's been going on. He's either out, or he's working on his computer in his room, or else he's on the phone. Maybe the only thing he's picked up on is that his father no longer gives him money as easily as he used to.

Rawan doesn't find her mom in the kitchen making lunch, like she usually does at this time of day. She must be outside somewhere. Rawan heads towards her room to dump her things and change her clothes. The phone rings several times before she's able to pick it up. Her sweater is stuck on her head, and she can't get it off. She passes the receiver under the sweater and is about to answer, but then stops. She hears a woman's voice on the other end saying, "I'm worried about you. I'm checking to make sure you're okay. Have you told your family yet?" Then a voice Rawan knows all too well answers—her dad's. She hadn't smelled his cigarette smoke when she first came home. She didn't even know he was here.

"No, I don't dare tell them anything yet. But I'll do it soon. I don't know how they'll react."

"I think they'll accept how things are now. Don't worry, this too shall pass," the female voice comforts him.

Rawan pulls the receiver away from her ear. She doesn't want to hear any more. She can't believe what she's hearing. She's stuck in her stubborn sweater, with the receiver still in her hand. She doesn't know what to do. Should she hang up? But then he might hear the click and find out she was eavesdropping the whole time. Rawan feels herself sweating buckets, her heart racing. Her head is spinning. She grasps the receiver, and it almost slips out of her hand because it's so sweaty. She regains her composure and raises the phone to her ear again, horrified by what she might hear next. Thankfully, all she hears is "*toooot.*" The female speaker, who had revealed why her father had started acting differently all of a sudden, had hung up. *He's definitely seeing another woman.*

Rawan sets the phone down on the floor. She grabs at the sweater on her head with both hands and pulls with all her might. She feels the woolen threads rip apart, one after the other. She keeps on pulling and pulling until she's shredded the whole sweater. Now, she can pass it around her waist, not just her head. Rawan holds the sweater and flings it to the ground. She stares at it, her gaze both victorious and spiteful. This beautiful, colorful woolen sweater that she had insisted on buying because she had fallen in love with it, even though it was too tight around her neck. This sweater that always fought her when she tried to put it on or take it off—it won't bother her anymore after today. It will no longer be an important piece of clothing in her closet. Here it is: torn apart, broken, injured, bleeding colored threads in all directions.

Only a few moments later, Rawan's gaze of victory and contempt turns to one of endless sadness. She hugs what is left of this sweater that bore the brunt of her anger, as if it were behind everything that's happening. She buries her face in it and sobs.

UNPLEASANT SURPRISE

ON MONDAY, when Ghady gets to school, he doesn't know what to expect from Michael. Will Thomas tell him what happened on Friday when Ghady was over at his house? If he does, will that make Michael's bullying even worse?

Ghady doesn't have to wait long for answers. He steps out of class at the afternoon break and is walking alone, looking for a friend, when Larry comes up. Larry holds Ghady's arm so nobody can see and whispers: "Follow me."

Ghady follows. If he refuses, it's just going to give Michael another chance to mock him for being a coward. He shakes his arm out of Larry's grip and walks beside him until they get to the gym. Ghady's surprised: as soon as he gets close to the group, he's surrounded. Sam, Andy, and Larry circle him so that he can't escape. Then Michael steps up and puts a joint in Ghady's mouth, whether he wants it or not. Ghady tries to defend himself, to slip away, but the boys are stronger than him, and they won't let him leave until he's smoked with them. Ghady takes a drag from the wet cigarette still in Michael's grip. Then Ghady pushes past the boys and falls down, the joint slipping from between his lips and landing on the ground. Michael snaps it up.

"Are you with us or what?" he says. "It's easy, just like you saw with Thomas. And it feels good. Am I right? So bring twenty euro, and I'll give you a bunch of these joints."

Ghady stands up. Now that he finds himself free of the boys' hands, he starts to run away from them, their high-pitched laughter striking his ears like bullets.

That night, when he's alone in his room, Ghady slides a rap CD into his stereo. He puts on his headphones and pushes the volume all the way up. He sits on his bed. Crying. He's still in shock from what happened to him two days ago, at Thomas's, and now *today*. He's still trying to take it in.

He pictures everything that happened: Was it for real? Thomas played this game to tighten their grip on him even more. He betrayed Ghady's trust.

So the boys are smoking dope at school—what should he do? Should he tell his parents so they'll report it to the school principal? No. What if Michael finds out? He will definitely get his revenge. Should he tell Rawan that things have gotten worse since what happened at Thomas's? No. Definitely not. That will just give her a bad idea of his school and of him. Although maybe things are already over between them, since she hasn't answered his last message. The idea of losing his friendship with Rawan scares him. Should he tell Zeina? No. He doesn't want her to come with her friends and defend him.

Ghady stops the music and picks up his oud. He adjusts the strings and starts to play the songs he's been learning the last two weeks. He plays fiercely. He plays until his fingers buzz from the pressure of the strings, since he's forgotten to use a pick. He gets tired. Stops playing.

But sleep doesn't come easily that night. Ghady tosses and turns on his mattress. He kicks the covers and throws them on the floor, only to pick them up again to cover himself from head to toe. He does this a couple of times before he finally drifts off.

In the morning, as soon as he opens his eyes, Ghady remembers what happened yesterday. The idea of going back to school scares him. Michael and his group might grab him again. He shakes his head and says to himself: *But I shouldn't be scared, even if there are a lot of them. I have friends, too.*

CONFUSION AND WORRY

THAT DAY, RAWAN doesn't leave her room. She stays there until nighttime, her closed eyes able to catch only an hour or two of sleep. She doesn't dare venture out and bump into her dad. She doesn't want to hug or kiss him like she usually does. She doesn't know how to face him, how to look at him, or what to say. Should she yell in his face and share all the anger that is burning inside her? Should she tell him that the way she feels about him changed in a matter of seconds—after he had been the best father she could've ever asked for, after she couldn't even express exactly how much she loved him? Or should she beg him to reconsider any decision that might destroy and scatter her family?

Rawan also doesn't want to see her mom. When her mom comes into the room telling Rawan it's time to eat, Rawan gives her a sideways glance, making it clear that she is busy reading her book. She says that she ate at school, feels tired, and just wants to lie down and sleep.

Rawan doesn't dare look into her mom's eyes. She's afraid her mom will read her thoughts. Her mom is amazing at that. She has this uncanny ability to pull information out of her, even when Rawan is trying to hide it. Rawan feels for her and is afraid of how shocked her mother will be. She won't tell her anything now. She'll wait to see what happens. But she asks herself, *Is it possible Mama already knows?*

Rawan sits at her desk and decides to write to Ghady, her friend who she needs now more than ever. He's the only one of her friends who knows what her family dynamics are really like. He'll understand why she feels the way she does, and he'll try to help her out. But should she tell him everything? She hesitates, then opens her email. She finds a message from him waiting and starts to read it, hoping it will cheer her up a little. But to her dismay, his email ties her stomach in more knots.

Monday, December 8, 2008

My dear friend,

Close to my heart, but far away, and sometimes stupid, Ghady . . . It seems we're both having problems at the same time. I'm surprised by what you wrote about weed in your email. For a second, I thought you were kidding. I honestly can't believe you would even think about trying it. I know you pretty well, which is why I'm surprised. Even though your new adventures make me worry, I'm happy because at least you told me what happened, and I feel better about the whole thing because you admit it was wrong and said you won't do it again. Please Ghady, stay away from Thomas so he can't pressure you again. Otherwise, I might end up annoyed with you forever, my sometimes-stupid friend.

On my end, I'm anxious and tired because, for a while now, I can feel that there's a rift between my parents. It's started to change the atmosphere in the house, and it's affecting me personally, too. I'll give you the details later.

I'm waiting for your reply. Tell me what's up with you.

Rawan

WHAT NOW?

GHADY STEPS ONTO THE playground and his heart
freezes. Even though he's trying to be tough, he feels scared. He doesn't
look right or left. He keeps his eyes fixed on the ground, moving
between the other students until he gets to his classroom. As soon as he
steps inside, his eyes meet Thomas's, who points to his pocket and tips
his head, as if asking if he has brought the twenty euros. Ghady is so
disappointed in his alleged friend! He ignores him and sits down in his
place beside Daniel. And when the class starts, Ghady tries to focus on
the math lesson, even though he can't hear anything. All he can think
about is this day being over.

And that isn't happening. At the afternoon break, Thomas comes up
to him: "What's with you, Ghady? You're not a total coward, are you?
Michael's not so bad. He just wants you to share . . . you know what.
Right?"

"Share the pot? And that I buy from him? That I smoke up like you
and sell to the younger kids?"

"Now you understand me." Thomas smiles widely, as if he means
well. "It's not hard, and seriously, it's no big deal. Plus, we score some
money in this really easy way."

"Were you doing this same stuff in your country before you came
here?" Ghady asks nervously. "Did you get expelled for it?"

"Don't be rude," Thomas says, even more nervously. "I've been really
patient with you. Come with me and don't be a snitch."

Before Ghady can figure out what's happening, he's surrounded by Michael and his group of ninth-grade boys. He looks around, hoping to see the playground supervisor. There he is. Close by. Ghady hopes he can still escape this mess.

"Seems like you only understand force," Michael whispers in his ear, plucking at the top of Ghady's sleeve. "If you don't bring the cash tomorrow, there's going to be hell to pay."

The boys scatter fast, before the supervisor notices. Ghady stays where he is, thinking, *Why me?*

Why is Michael picking on him? Because he's a racist and hates him? And Thomas? Why is he taking advantage of their friendship? And what if this gets out? He does have more than twenty euros—maybe fifty, since he's been saving up for a cell phone. If he goes along with them, then he'll be free, and they will stop bugging him. Plus, people say marijuana is less harmful than nicotine or smoking a *shisha* pipe. Ohhh . . . . He's about to cry from how scared and angry he is.

"Is there a problem?"

It's the voice of the playground supervisor, walking up to him. Ghady shakes free of his thoughts, which he'll save for some other time.

"No, no," he hurriedly answers, imagining the supervisor can read his mind. Then he walks over to the clusters of students. Daniel sees him and heads in his direction. Ghady gets ahold of himself and suppresses his tears.

"What's up? What did Michael want?"

Ghady doesn't say anything. He really doesn't want to drag Daniel into this. He touches his friend's shoulder, his lips tight and the muscles in his face tense. Together, they walk to the cafeteria.

That night, Ghady decides to tell his sister what's going on.

NOTHING MATTERS

THE NEXT MORNING, Rawan crawls out of bed, tired. She looks at her face in the mirror. Her eyes are puffy, ringed by dark circles. Some new pimples have popped up on her forehead. She doesn't care about washing her face with her special soap like she usually would. She touches her skin and thinks, *Let the pimples camp out and fill my entire face. Nothing matters anymore. I won't even brush my hair today. I'll leave it bushy, sticking out in all directions, scattered like my thoughts. What's going to happen? Who's going to care?*

At school, Rawan's friends pick up on this change. In Chemistry, the teacher reprimands her for not finishing the homework exercises. Rawan responds with a disregard that shocks everyone in her class. "I don't even like Chemistry. I mean, what's the point of learning it? I'm not going to be a doctor or a pharmacist or a chemistry teacher when I'm older."

"I want to see you at the end of class, Rawan," the teacher says curtly.

In the schoolyard, after her meeting with the teacher, Raed asks her, out of concern, "What happened? What did she say to you?"

"She gave me a verbal warning," Rawan says with a strange, sarcastic grin. "She said she'll call my parents if I act out like that again." She falls silent for a moment, then adds, "As if what I've got going on at home isn't enough!"

"Did something else happen, Rawan? We all feel like there's something dragging you down. *Chérie*, tell me, maybe we can help," Karen suggests. "The problem is too big," Rawan declares, her voice wavering between frustration and despair. "I don't think anyone can help me."

All her friends stay silent for a while, watching their downcast friend. Trying to change the atmosphere, Noor says, "Come on now, we miss the fun and funny Rawan, where is she? Being sad won't change a thing. I know! Why don't you focus on your campaign? People won't vote for someone who's down in the dumps. You'd better watch it, because if you keep on acting like this, you're going to boost my chances of winning. Giving up so soon, huh? Don't you want to take me on? I'm trying to be humble—we all know I'm going to win anyway, but I just don't want it to be *this* easy." She smiles. "Where's the fun if there's no competition?"

"Honestly, the class elections don't matter to me anymore. Nothing matters. Not even drawing."

At this, Raed interjects, "Not even delicious food? Let me tell you about the *kishk* my mom made yesterday, and on top of that there were potato cubes and *qawarma* . . . Mmm."

Maya cuts him off. "Who can say no to *qawarma*? Welcome back to Chef Raed's show that always makes our tongues tingle. If only one day you'd invite us over to taste all these dishes that you keep telling us about, instead of forcing us to imagine them. We also want to eat, Raed. Stop teasing us, please!" All the friends laugh, but this doesn't succeed in bringing a smile, even just a small one, to Rawan's face. She remains silent and distracted.

WORST-CASE SCENARIO

"I HAVE TO TELL YOU something important," Ghady starts. "But *please*, Zeina, I don't want you to get involved, and I don't want you to tell Mom or your friends. And please don't go telling the principal."

"At your service, Sir. But now you're scaring me. What is it?"

"You know Michael in ninth grade? The one who doesn't go anywhere without his gang: Sam and Larry and Andy?"

"Did you get hurt? Did they attack you?"

"Not exactly . . . . They smoke pot at school, and . . . "

"Sure. It's common knowledge in my class, and Michael's really scared of the older boys. But how come you know about it?"

"That's the problem. They wanted me to join them, and—"

"And then what? Of course you didn't agree to it . . . Did you?"

"Don't worry, Zeina. If I'd joined them, I wouldn't be coming to tell you about it. But they're serious about this, and they keep on pressuring me. Honestly, I'm scared of them."

"You have to go tell the administration right away, Ghady. These guys are dangerous."

"You know that if I go to the administration, they'll accuse me of being with them. Then I'll get in trouble, too—and I don't deserve it. Or maybe they'll believe me and punish Michael's gang . . . and that would be worse. Because then he'll hate me even more, and he'll have even more reasons to bully me."

"Stop it, Ghady. You're always like this, imagining the worst so you can avoid confrontation. Michael is definitely going to be expelled when they find out about this. You'll just have to be brave, and then you can feel good about it for the rest of your life."

"Forget it, Zeina. I wish I hadn't told you."

"And what do you suggest? Just take their abuse? Stick your hands in your pockets and do nothing?"

"I don't know. But you can't go to the principal. Promise me!"

"Fine. But on the condition that you go, and that you stay away from those weasels."

"I promise . . . But seriously, I'm scared of them. There's a lot of them, and they're all stronger than me."

"Don't be dumb. Don't you see how tall and muscular you are? You shouldn't be scared of anyone."

"You don't know these guys."

"I know them well enough. And don't forget what Mom always says about strength. It comes from within. If they see that you're scared, then they're going to use that. Walk confidently and don't pay them any attention."

"I know what Mom says. As far as she's concerned, all I have to do is look them straight in the eye and say in a firm voice that they're bothering me. Poor Mom. She has no clue what things are like at school. She doesn't know that sometimes the playground is more like a jungle than a place to play. And she definitely doesn't know that the supervisors are so busy watching for stupid things—like someone throwing a ball and hitting a window, or dropping a piece of paper on the ground—that they don't notice the real problems, like smoking or beating up on the younger kids."

"You're right about that," Zeina says, before she hears them being called to the dining room for the third time. Time for dinner.

"Shh!" Ghady whispers. "Not a word."

"As you command," Zeina whispers, giving an exaggerated gesture that makes Ghady laugh for the first time that day.

Ghady feels a little less anxious after talking with his sister. He decides that tonight he'll answer Rawan's latest letter.

Tuesday, December 16, 2008

Rawan,

It's been a week since I wrote you. I'm really sorry, but I know you'll forgive me when you hear the reason. I mean, of course I'm busy with school, and the reading and studying and all, but I have other problems at school . . . that are really serious. I'll tell you everything when I see you. Seriously, God knows how I'm going to make it through this year. But don't worry about my stuff too much. I promise I'll take care of myself and I won't do anything stupid.

Are things really that bad with your parents? I don't believe it! I've known them since I was little, and I can't imagine them fighting. I hope they patch things up really soon. Now I understand why you haven't been feeling well lately.

What's your other news? What about your school and activities? I don't even know if you were elected this year's student representative for your class. Did it happen? And what about your drawing? Surely you've become a master artist. ☺ I can't wait to see your art work, Ms. Rawan.

The thing that makes me happy these days is playing the oud. When I play, I release all my anger, just like you told me to. My lessons are okay. Not excellent, but good, and I'm definitely going to work harder this year. In three days, we'll have Christmas break. Three weeks of freedom and sleeping till noon! I might go with my family on a trip to Seville in southern Spain. I'm really excited about it, and I can practice speaking Spanish, because I'm learning that in school, too. Did I tell you? Anyway, what are you doing over the break? I remember you said you had to do a lot of schoolwork over vacation. I hope I'm wrong.

I have to go now.

Don't take a long time to answer like I did . . . I'm waiting for your reply, and tell Jad hi.

Love,
Ghady

PINK SHOES

RAWAN WAKES UP EARLY. She remembers Ghady. Then she logs onto her account and reads his latest message. *What a coincidence. Ghady and I are both having problems at the same time, and we both need someone to stand by and support us, even if it's only moral support.* She writes:

Thursday, December 18, 2008

My friend,

I decided to answer your email as soon as I finished reading it. I hope that your problems get solved soon, Ghady. I'm worried about you. I don't know what you mean by really serious problems, but I hope they're not the kind that make you dizzy and lose your mind. You said that you would tell me more when you see me. Does that mean I'll have to wait all the way until summer vacation? Do you think I can wait that long? Anyhow, I'm trusting that you won't do anything else stupid.

As for what's happening between my parents, it's the same, or maybe even worse. The elections for class representative are right before the holiday break. I don't feel psyched for it anymore. Even my drawing lessons—I don't enjoy them as much as I used to.

Wow, the holidays start tomorrow for you guys! Ours start in a week. How unfair. Obviously my teachers are going to drown us in tons of homework as usual. ☹

I can't wait for the vacation. I plan to spend most of it with my grandma. I feel more relaxed at her place, and it will be good for me to spend some time away from the drama at home.

I hope you have an awesome time in Seville. Think of me when you're devouring that delicious paella! Don't take too long to write back. I have to get ready for school now, it's almost 7:30!

Bye . . .

Your friend,

Rawan

Rawan steps into the schoolyard convinced that the principal, Ms. Salwa, will comment on her bushy hair and pink shoes. Her shoes and school uniform clash, but she decided to wear them anyway.

Rawan feels Ms. Salwa's eyes on her, following her around the yard. The principal enjoys grabbing—or more like "arresting"—students who break school rules. She also loves scolding them; it's her favorite pastime. She never smiles, and her face is always stern, to the point that the kids call her "Cop Salwa."

Many times, Rawan has wondered how Ms. Salwa expresses joy. She tries to imagine her laughing out loud at a joke or a funny movie.

And now here she comes. Rawan steadies herself for the string of observations about what's wrong with her, and mentally prepares herself to go home and change her shoes if she's asked to do it. The last thing she expects is Ms. Salwa kindly putting a hand on her shoulder and saying with a warm smile, "Rawan, you know full well that this color isn't allowed. Don't wear those shoes to school ever again, and please tie your hair up. Your face is prettier when we can see it." *I can't believe it. Ms. Salwa is actually smiling at me. I must be dreaming.*

As it turns out, Ms. Salwa isn't the only one who has become kind all of a sudden. It's as if kindness had suddenly become mandatory for all her teachers and classmates, especially when it comes to Rawan. Instead of the Chemistry teacher putting her down for a bad grade, she gives Rawan a few words of encouragement. She also says that the grade will be thrown out if Rawan does better next time. Her Geography teacher doesn't lay into her when she tells him that she hasn't done her homework, but instead tells her to turn it in later in the week. And before the English teacher leaves the room, she gives Rawan a reassuring pat and whispers in her ear, "Be strong, Rawan. We all go through difficult patches, and . . . "

Rawan doesn't hear the rest of the sentence—she feels a coldness spread through her body. Now she understands why everyone is being so nice to her: they all know about her problem. She suddenly feels embarrassed and uncomfortable. She looks into the eyes of the other kids in the class, hoping to figure out who knows what and who's pitying her. In that moment, Rawan wishes she could just disappear, run out of class, far away from the stares she feels are following her. She imagines what everyone must think. Poor Rawan . . . her parents are getting a divorce . . . her family is falling apart . . . poor girl . . . what will happen to her?

During the ten o'clock break, she heads for her friends and asks them outright, "Have any of you told someone what I told you?" Everyone says no except Noor. Rawan turns to her angrily. "Noor—did you tell someone about my parents? It feels like everyone knows: the principal, the teachers, even the other kids."

Noor bows her head and avoids Rawan's steady gaze. "I told the English teacher because she asked why you were falling behind all of a sudden. She knows we're friends. I wanted to help and explain what was happening with you, and . . . I told Nadine, too. She also asked what was up with you. She promised she wouldn't tell anyone. That big-mouth. Why did I ever trust her? Rawan, I'm sorry. I had no idea it would spread like wildfire, I'm really sorry."

Hearing Noor's answer, Rawan explodes. Her friends can't manage to calm her down. She, herself, almost can't believe what she's saying. Angry words, thoughtless words. She yells in Noor's face, "You're just jealous because I have a family and I live with my mom and dad in the same house. You must have been happy when you found out my parents were separating, just like yours, so you hurried up and spread the news near and far." She finishes her rant with a single menacing sentence: "You're not my friend and I never want to speak to you again."

Noor looks at Rawan with tears in her eyes and moves far away.

Rawan falls silent. She feels like she's woken up from a dream. No— more like a nightmare. Her final sentence echoes loudly in her ears. She feels embarrassed when she looks at her friends' faces, and they look at her reproachfully, their gazes heavy with blame. *I really didn't have to say all that. I went overboard.* In a flash, her feelings seesaw. *No, she deserved it. She wasn't supposed to tell anyone. I can be understanding, but she's the one who made the mistake in the first place. A real friend doesn't spill your secrets.*

That day, Rawan tells her friends that she's decided to withdraw from the elections. When asked why, she gives the excuse that she's busy with schoolwork and wants to pull her grades up, which means she can't take on any new responsibilities.

But the truth is she doesn't want a pity vote from her friends because of what she's going through. And after what happened between Noor and her, the whole thing would be awkward. They'd have to choose between the two of them, and their vote would be like standing with one girl and against the other. Rawan doesn't want to be put in such an uncomfortable and difficult position. Her current issues are more than she can handle.

TO SEVILLE

FOR SOME REASON, GHADY doesn't see Michael at school in the last two days before Christmas and New Year's break. There is no trace of him on the playground, although he spots Michael's group of followers from time to time. In the absence of their "leader," they don't come up to him. The two days pass peacefully for Ghady, and, on Friday evening, he and his family go to the airport—to Seville!

During the vacation in Seville, Ghady forgets his problems at school, at least for a while. But for some reason, whenever he sees a boy on the street or sidewalk who looks like he's smoking pot, he imagines it's Michael. One day, as he's walking in a garden with Zeina while their parents are out shopping, he tells her: "Do you know that, wherever I look, I see boys like Michael? At first glance, I think maybe he's really come to Spain."

"Maybe because there are a lot of English tourists here, and he's English," his sister says.

"What if he really is here with his family?" Ghady asks, adding quickly: "But no. It's not possible."

"Why isn't it possible?" Zeina asks.

"Matthias lives across the street from Michael, and he told me that Michael lives with only his mom, and he hardly ever goes on vacation with her. Sometimes he goes to visit his dad in London. Matthias said Michael's mom travels a lot, and, when she does, Michael stays at home by himself. Money isn't a problem, and she gives him all the cash he needs, so he won't keep calling while she's away. Michael doesn't like visiting his dad—his parents separated when he was just three. His mom says his dad was violent and abusive, so she left him."

"What, are you opening an investigation? You have a lot of information, boy!"

Ghady laughs. "I have friends. That's all there is to it."

"Now I feel sorry for Michael. His life definitely hasn't been easy."

"Don't be weird, Zeina. How can you feel sorry for him? He's a bad person."

As they walk, Ghady and Zeina find an internet café.

"Let's go in," Ghady says. "I want to check my email. Do you have any cash?"

"Just seven euros. I think it's enough."

Ghady reads the prices on the coffee shop's glass front: "Two euros an hour."

That's enough money for the internet and a small glass of juice for each of them.

As soon as Ghady opens his mailbox, his head starts thudding and his face goes red. It's a message from Michael. He wrote only a few words.

Tuesday December 23, 2008

I'm right behind you. Did you think you could run away, coward? Show me you're a man and meet me behind the gym during lunch on the first day back after break. Michael.

Ghady doesn't answer the letter, but he doesn't delete it.

There's another one from Rawan, and he writes a quick reply.

Tuesday December 23, 2008

My dear friend,

I want to wish you a Merry Christmas and a Happy New Year! I'm in Spain right now, with Zeina and my mom and dad. You should come visit this country—it's really beautiful. The people look like us, and their music even sounds like ours. They call it "flamenco."

All my love,
Ghady

ESCAPE

RAWAN ARRIVES home. She eats lunch with her parents, and, as has been usual lately, responds to their questions without really thinking. They are always the same questions. "How was your day? Any grades you want to share? Do you have a lot of work for tomorrow?" The questions are followed by a long, dreary silence that lasts until the end of the meal.

Rawan has started getting used to the clear tension between her parents, which is broken up now and then by annoying chitchat about stuff that doesn't even matter.

Later that afternoon, something new happens, adding a thrill to the household's boring routine. While she is in her room, staring at the pages of her book, Rawan hears her father's voice bellowing in the room next to hers. "Every day, it's 'I want money, I want money.' What do you do with all the money you take, Rani? Isn't it enough that I'm paying your sky-high college fees? Do you know what most people your age are doing? They're working to make their own money and paying their own way through college. And what do you do? You go out with your friends and spend all your time having fun and bleeding my money dry. When I was your age, I was working to support my parents! Go on! Find a job, then maybe you'll finally understand the value of hard work." Rawan is surprised to hear no comeback from her brother. *Maybe he's so shocked he can't speak. Baba, who always spoils him and gives in to whatever he wants, is asking him to work! Baba, who used to push back if Mama even asked Rani to carry his plate to the kitchen or hang up his clothes. I wonder what has changed. Is he trying to cut down on our costs here at home so he can save up for his new life? With someone else?*

Rawan freezes as this idea buds inside her head. Things are becoming clearer, little by little, and what's strange is that she might be the only one who knows what is going on.

The next morning, Rawan walks into the schoolyard and makes her way to the oak tree. She waves at her friends and notices that Noor isn't with them. She's a little relieved, because she doesn't know how she would act if she saw Noor again. Feelings of regret over what happened yesterday needle at her. She couldn't control her temper when talking to Noor, who, unfortunately for her, had to deal with the fury that's been bubbling inside Rawan for weeks—like lava just waiting to erupt.

The bell rings. Rawan walks into the classroom with her friends. She sees Noor come in without looking in her direction. *She must have come late. It looks like she didn't sleep well. She looks wiped. Obviously what I said yesterday must have hurt and kept her awake.* Another idea creeps into Rawan's mind. *Whatever, staying up late is good for her. Maybe it gave her a chance to think about what she did to me. Thanks to her, everyone here knows my story. It might as well have been printed in the school paper.*

The final days before vacation pass as dull and normal as can be. Rawan doesn't talk to Noor, and she doesn't congratulate her for being elected class representative. Her friends attempt to convince Rawan to move on and talk to Noor, but fail. Raed suggests leaving it now and coming back to it after the break, which will give Rawan time to get over her family crisis or at least make her peace with it.

Rawan spends most of her holiday at her grandma's. She enjoys playing backgammon and helping her grandmother cook the delicious dishes she loves, like *mujaddara* with cabbage, Rawan's all-time favorite. It reminds her of the time when she and Rani spent the summer with their grandma when their parents went on holiday.

I used to love staying at grandma's, but I would miss my parents too much and wished they would hurry up and come back. Now they're both in Lebanon and I'm far away from both of them, which is exactly what I want right now. Seeing them stresses me out, and their cold war is upsetting.

That day, Rawan heads home to pick up her clothes and some other stuff. She throws her parents and her brother a quick "hi." Her brother jokes, "You've become a guest here, Mademoiselle Rawan, only coming to get your stuff, I see. We've missed you, haven't you missed us?" In a soft voice, avoiding their eyes, she answers, "It's not like that. I've

79

missed you guys, too, but I'm more comfortable at Grandma's, and she needs someone to keep her entertained. I've decided to stay there until the end of the break. I've got a lot of homework, you know, and the atmosphere there is better for studying." Her parents exchange looks. "Whatever you want *habibti*, tell Grandma I say hi," her mother says.

Before leaving the house, Rawan checks her email. She reads Ghady's letter and responds.

Tuesday, December 30, 2008

Dear Ghady,

Hello, my friend. I've only just read your email because I've been spending most of my time at my grandma's, and she doesn't have internet. I have more fun at her place. I discovered that, right now, I really need someone as kind and soft as she is with me. I feel so much better with her. Of course, I haven't told her anything, because I don't want to worry her. In a few days, my holiday will be over, and I'll have to go home, even though that is the last thing I want. I can't explain this feeling that gets under my skin.

I'm so happy that you had a great time in Seville with your family. Ghady, I hope you have a great year, full of joy and melodies . . .

I'll be waiting for your reply.

Best wishes,
Rawan

EVEN MATTHIAS?

GHADY DOESN'T GO see Michael on the first day back, as he's been ordered. Most of the time, he stays with his friends and avoids being alone on the playground. The school day passes all right . . . until it's time to go home. Ghady walks to the school's front gate to meet his mom, who's coming from work as usual. But before he gets to her car, he sees Michael. It seems like Michael has been watching him.

Michael walks up and pushes his face right up against Ghady's. "Tomorrow. That's your last chance to bring the 20 euros. Don't be stubborn. It doesn't make any sense to resist—well, except you seem to be the type who likes problems. Your friend Matthias is smarter than you are. He brought the money today and we gave him . . . you know what. Ha."

Ghady is stunned. Matthias? Did they threaten him, too? Michael's acting like he is the leader of a gang.

Ghady shifts into a voice he tries to make more adult than his boyish vocal cords will allow: "What if I say no?"

"I have friends . . . and strength. Don't make me use it."

"I have friends, too."

"Hahaha! You mean Daniel? That idiot's not going to help you. All he can do is read through his thick glasses."

"Don't talk about him like that. He's my best friend and the smartest kid in the class."

"You know how I'm sure he's stupid? He chose *you* as a friend." Michael laughs.

Ghady is so angry he's on the verge of losing his temper and throwing himself on Michael with all his strength, just to teach him a lesson. But he holds back. His mom drives up and, as she sits there behind the wheel, signals for him to get in the car. He runs his palms over his curly hair, which has gotten really long. Then he takes a deep breath and walks away from Michael, toward the car.

"Who's that boy?" his mom asks. "He looks older than you."

"It's Michael from ninth grade," Ghady says, just as Zeina is climbing into the car. His sister starts talking with their mom, changing the subject. Ghady sighs. It's like his mom doesn't even remember what happened with Michael and his oud. Ghady sinks into his thoughts.

At school the next day, as soon as he sees Matthias, he takes him aside to find out what he knows about Michael.

"Michael brings the stuff to school—I've seen him taking baggies out of his pocket. Whenever he gets a chance, he'll catch one of the younger students and try to get them to smoke. I said I'd try after he pressured me a lot of times. Honestly, I just wanted him to stop."

"Matthias! You're crazy. What if they find out you're doing this at school? Or what if you get addicted?"

"Seriously, Ghady, don't overreact! Let me finish. When boys agree to smoke with him, he tells them to bring in money to buy it."

"And that's what happened to you?"

"Ahhh . . . almost," Matthias says, like he's embarrassed to answer. "When I brought him the twenty euros, Michael gave me a little bit in a baggie and taught me how to roll it."

"Bravo!" Ghady claps his hands to underline how ridiculous all this is.

"Seriously, though, Ghady, it's not going to help if you're stubborn. I mean, if you just go along with it, then they'll leave you alone."

"No way! We shouldn't let them drag us into this. It's dangerous, plus I don't want any problems. And I *definitely* don't want my parents to find out. I only have one more week left to save up, and then I'll have enough for a phone! I don't want to spend all my money on something dumb just so Michael and his friends will leave me alone."

"A phone? Why doesn't your dad just buy you one? Come on, don't be so lame. Your parents aren't going to know if you buy a little bit. I mean, just buy it and throw it in the trash."

"My parents don't find cash on the street so I can throw it away like that."

At the break, after one period of English and two math classes where he can't focus, Ghady sits on a bench on the playground next to Daniel, who's reading the latest *Harry Potter*.

"Michael's waiting for you—you know where—behind the far building." Andy's voice is behind him.

Ghady thinks for a second. He looks at Daniel to see his reaction. Nothing. He's lost in his book.

Could Ghady just blow him off? "And who told you I'm going to do what your boss wants?"

Andy says nothing. He just backs off and disappears. A few minutes later, it isn't Andy standing in front of Ghady, but Michael.

CHOCOLATE

IT'S THE FIRST DAY back at school after the break. The friends huddle together and share stories about what they did over the holiday. Rawan listens to them silently, her eyes heavy with a noticeable sadness. Karen sighs and says, "As soon as the vacation starts, it's over. Time flies when you're having fun. *Quel dommage!*" She turns to Rawan and asks, "How was your break? I hope you got to relax and that things are better between your parents."

After Karen's question, Rawan feels that everyone is watching her, waiting for an answer, as if each of them wants to ask their own question, but doesn't dare to. She looks at them and doesn't answer. "We just want to make sure you're okay, Rawan. Anything new?" Raed asks.

"Things are still the same, but I got away from it all by staying at my grandma's over the break. I relaxed there for a bit. To be honest, I wish I was still there. I didn't call you guys, but I needed some time away, some time to myself."

That day passes like any other, both at school and at home. Classes and assignments at school, and the usual suffocating silence at home.

The next day, Rawan opens her backpack to take out her pencil case and suddenly comes across a small box, wrapped up and tied with a colorful ribbon. She looks around, astonished. Where did this box come from? It wasn't in her bag this morning. She'd put her bag down on the ground in the corner of the schoolyard before making her way to the oak tree. She wonders who opened her bag and put this in. *Was it put there by mistake?* Rawan doesn't dare to open it in class. She can't stop thinking about it, and she can't wait for the end of morning classes to find out what's inside this mysterious box. Everyone streams outside during break, but she stays back, with the excuse that she needs to organize her desk. She opens the box to find pieces of hazelnut chocolate. She remembers her parents' and teachers' repeated warnings about not taking anything from strangers. She feels reassured when she searches the box and finds it completely sealed. The chocolate is carefully wrapped, and it's also a well-known brand.

This small, unexpected gift succeeds in lifting Rawan's spirits. She feels joy make its way into her heart, taking the place of the worry that had taken root there for a while now.

She decides not to tell anyone about the gift, because whoever gave it to her would surely reveal their identity soon enough. *Maybe it's from Noor? Is she trying to say sorry?*

Rawan quickly exits the classroom, heading to the schoolyard, where she crashes into Husam, a ninth grader. She apologizes. He looks at her and jokes, "Thank God no one got injured! Next time be more careful when you're driving, Miss." Rawan laughs and edges away, thinking, *What a cutie!* Then she whispers to herself, patting her shoulder tenderly, "Argh. It hurts a little."

The gift's effect on Rawan lasts for the whole day. She greets Noor, who responds coldly and avoids any further conversation, which makes Rawan think the gift can't be from her.

When Rawan opens her bag the next day, she's surprised to find another wrapped box inside. Later on, she finds that inside is a beautifully decorated mug with 'You're Special' written on it in multicolored letters. Rawan can't think anymore. Questions crowd her head. *Who gave me this? What do they want from me? Why not give it in person?*

She looks around. Maybe she can solve this mystery that's been keeping her so busy. Whoever gave her the gifts must be someone close to her, someone who knows her well.

She considers Husam, who comes up to her. "How are you doing today?" he says. "Do you know my shoulder's still sore because of what happened yesterday? I should ask for compensation. I'd be happy with a nice bar of chocolate. What do you think?"

Hearing the word chocolate, Rawan freezes, even though she'd had a response ready to go about her own shoulder pains. Her words catch in her throat. She blushes, feeling confused. She stammers, "Choco-late!

Oh . . . " Husam chuckles and adds, as he walks on, "Okay, okay. Don't worry! I won't ask for anything. I didn't think you'd get so flustered. I was just kidding, just kidding."

Rawan returns home, ideas whizzing back and forth in her head. *Could it be that Husam put those gifts in my bag? But why me? Was it just a coincidence that he was outside my class yesterday? Was his asking for chocolate just a coincidence? Of course not. He must like me, and he's trying to tell me in his own special way. He's so charming!*

Her face gets hot when she remembers the conversation they had in the schoolyard. *It's possible that Husam is the mastermind behind all this. And then what do I do? I stutter, unable to get out two words, and he thinks I can't even part with a bar of chocolate! Maybe now he thinks I'm stingy.*

Rawan decides to let Ghady know what's going on with her. He's the only friend who won't spill her secrets. Ghady's a boy, and he knows how guys think. He'll help her and give her some excellent tips.

Thursday, January 12, 2009

Dear Ghady,

How are you? I haven't heard anything from you in ages. What's happening? Does the saying, 'Out of sight, out of mind' now apply to you too? Have you forgotten about your friend in Beirut?

I'm doing fine. I want to tell you about something that has been going on for the past two days. I think I might have a secret admirer at school. I got two presents from someone, and I don't know who. I won't hide the fact that getting them brightened my day and made me giddy, but at the same time it set my mind buzzing. I've got someone specific in mind, but I'm confused about what to do. Should I ask him directly if he's the one who gave me the presents, or should I wait until I'm sure? What do you think?

So I've spilled the beans on my life. What about yours? What's happening with that problem in school? Has anything else happened that you haven't told me about? You better answer right away.

Rawan

THE FIGHT: 1

GHADY STANDS UP, ready for a confrontation.

"Aren't you coming, coward?"

"Can't you understand anything?" Ghady says sharply. "I don't want to buy from you."

"Sure, I understand now. You want to stick with other Arabs," Michael says in a provocative, ironic tone. "How come that didn't occur to me before?"

Anger creeps into Ghady's expression, but Michael doesn't seem to care. He goes on teasing him: "All you Arabs are terrorists, and—"

Ghady shouts in his face, warning him to get back: "Enough! You're an ignorant racist. Just leave me alone!"

Michael puts an arm out in front of Ghady, trying to block his path. Ghady shoves against the outstretched arm. "Get out of my way!" But as soon as he slips away from Michael's grasp, Michael steps toward him like a predator swooping down on an enemy. Then outrage explodes out of him!

A fierce fight breaks out between the boys. Other students gather around, some on Ghady's side and others cheering for Michael. Daniel is shocked. His book falls from his hands. He stays frozen in place, open-mouthed.

AGAIN, THE MIRROR

THAT EVENING, Rawan stares at her face in the mirror, something she hasn't done in a while. She washes her skin with the special soap that has started to dry out since she hasn't used it in so long. She decides to wake up early the next morning and make an effort with how she looks before heading off to school.

Rawan gets to the schoolyard with a new hairstyle—she's tied her curly hair over her head in a bun and stuck a beautiful comb through it. She puts her bag down to one side and makes her way to the oak tree.

Her friends ooh and ah. "What's this change? Your hair looks fab today, *très jolie!*" Karen gushes.

"With your hair like that we can finally get a clear look at your almond-shaped, honey-colored eyes. You've really outdone yourself Rawan!" Raed adds. The comments from Rawan's friends put her on cloud nine. Even Noor looks at her with a faint smile on her face. Maya looks at Raed and teases, "Even when you're complimenting someone, you're still thinking about food. Almond-shaped, honey-colored . . . what's next? Hazelnut hair?" Everyone cracks up, and Rawan laughs for what feels like the first time in ages.

But the whole time, she keeps an eye on her bag. She catches Husam entering the schoolyard. She waits a bit, and then she makes her way over to him, smiling, and says, "Good morning. I hope your shoulder is feeling better." She reaches into her jacket pocket and takes out some chocolate, "Here, I hope you like it." Husam takes the chocolate from her hand and titters. "Thanks, friend, even though I really was kidding. You look different today. The hairstyle suits you." His words make Rawan blush.

Before going to class, she unzips her bag and makes a show of looking for a tissue, but she doesn't find anything new in her backpack. She's disappointed for a few moments, then says to herself, *Don't be greedy now. What, do you want a gift every day?*

In Science, she puts her hand in her desk to take out the textbook and is startled to find a colored glass inside. She looks inside the glass and sees a white teddy bear with a purple ribbon around its neck. She is ecstatic, and her earlier feelings of disappointment wash away.

The days go by like this. Every so often, she discovers a small present in her desk, in the pocket of her jacket hanging in class, or in her bag: sweets, a beaded bracelet, a colored card, and a keychain. Despite her continued surveillance, she can't catch the secret admirer, who is a pro at hiding these small surprises for her without anyone catching him, even though she's pretty sure it's Husam.

Things get better for Rawan at school, even though nothing changes at home, which is still making her worry and draining her energy. At school, she is no longer sad like before, and her fun-loving spirit returns, little by little. She decides to take an interest in her grades again, and, more importantly, she starts to spend time fixing herself up in the mornings.

This improvement in her behavior makes her friends and teachers feel reassured about her situation. One day, Maya even tells her, "I hope things have gotten better between your parents. From how you've been acting, I feel like it must be better. You seem more relaxed." Here, Rawan seizes the opportunity to say, "Yes, things between them are much better now. I think I was wrong and was too quick to judge." Maya smiles and hugs her, saying, "How awesome!" Then she flutters off to tell her friends the good news.

I've finally set things straight. Pretty soon, this will spread like wildfire through the entire school. It will be enough if that big-mouth Nadine hears it. Ah, I feel so much better! Now I don't have to worry about their funny looks or what they're thinking whenever I pass by.

THE FIGHT: 2

THE TWO STRUGGLING boys charge at each other. Hard, random blows rain down on their bodies. The fight is ferocious, but it doesn't last long. The playground supervisor sees the group bunched together, and he runs to separate the fighters, yelling at them to stop. They pull themselves up off the ground, where they've been knocked by the intensity of the fight. Then the two of them follow the supervisor, who orders them to go with him to the principal's office.

Ghady walks slowly and heavily. His whole body aches, and blood is streaming from his lower lip. As for Michael, his hair is a mess and his shirt's ripped, but he walks confidently, as though he were in the right and Ghady had attacked *him*.

The principal listens to both of their stories. Ghady tells her about Michael's racist comments, and Michael insists he was attacked for no reason. After they finish, the principal speaks.

"Whatever your reasons, Ghady, we don't solve our problems with our fists. And as for you, Michael, this is hardly the first time you've been in a fight. It seems you have already forgotten your suspension during the last two days before break for hitting a fourth-grader. And you know that racist language is absolutely forbidden here at school. You have to show respect to all your fellow students."

Michael doesn't meet the principal's gaze. Instead, he stares at his fingernails, trying to scrape out the dirt that got underneath them during their fight.

The principal finishes: "Ghady, this is the first time you've made trouble for yourself, so I'm not going to punish you. But this has to be the first and last time I hear about any trouble from you."

She turns to Michael. "As for you, Michael, you've had more than enough chances this year. So these are the consequences of today's fight: This week and next, you are going to stay after school for an hour, cleaning the classrooms and shelving books in the library."

Michael shoots an angry, disgusted look at Ghady. "Can I go now?"

"Wait. I want to send a quick message to your mother. You, Ghady, go back to class."

Ghady walks out of the principal's office, thinking about everything that's happened. What he really needs now is to see Rawan and Jad. He hasn't answered Rawan's last two letters, even though he read them both the day they came. She definitely will be wondering what is going on with him. Definitely? Or maybe not. Maybe she's forgotten about him, and she's thinking only about the secret admirer who is leaving her presents. The idea makes him sad. Is he jealous? He's always thought of her as just a friend. But now . . . Where are these feelings coming from? Does he even have time for this? Should he tell her about today's fight? He knows she'll be supportive, but he doesn't want to burden her with his problems. She has enough to worry about with her family. Things don't seem okay with her . . . so, for now, he won't write her. He decides to wait a few days, until his nerves settle down a little.

THE SECRET OF CHANGE

RAWAN MAKES an important decision. She is going to tell Rani about their father. Maybe together they can find a solution to the problem.

She walks into the house to find her parents sitting with Rani in the living room. She says hello and is about to head for her room when she hears her father's voice say, "Rawan, come here, *habibti*, and have a seat. I want to talk to you all about something important." Rawan sits on the couch, her heart racing. She feels a coldness spread from her fingers up to her shoulders. *Okay,* she thinks, *this is it. He's going to tell us about how they're getting a divorce. Please God, don't let it happen, I'll do anything. I'll be better, I'll help the poor. Please God, please.*

Rawan's dad starts talking, his words directed at his wife. "First of all, I want to apologize for how I've been acting lately. I've been irritable and losing my temper for no reason. There is something I tried to hide from you all, but I'm going to come clean now, which will be better for all of us. Because of the economic crisis, the company I work for lost a lot of money, and the administration decided to lay off a number of employees. They started with some of the older employees who had larger salaries. Unfortunately, I was one of them, and it hasn't been easy for me to swallow." He falls silent for a few moments, then adds sadly, "In other words, I've been unemployed for a while, and we're going to go through a rough patch where we'll have to curb our spending until I can get a handle on things. I need your help and support."

Rawan's mother moves closer to her husband and hugs him while blaming him for not telling her everything from the start. Rani does the same and promises his dad to be more careful with his allowance and to not keep asking for stuff after today. He even promises to search for a job that will cover his expenses. As for Rawan, to everyone's utter surprise, she starts jumping for joy, waving her hands around while looking up and shouting, "Thank you God, thank you, thank you! I'll be a better person, I'll help the poor, thank you, THANK YOU." She then hugs her parents, tears streaming out of her eyes. Of course they're not tears of sadness.

Back in her room, Rawan logs onto her email. Nothing from Ghady. She writes a few words.

Thursday, February 19, 2009

Ghady, where are you? I didn't get any answer to my last two emails. Are you okay, Belgian Waffle? Have you drowned in the rain over there? Ha! I'm only writing to let you know that today is the happiest day of my life. I won't tell you any more for now . . . this is the new Rawan way of keeping you on the edge of your seat.

Stop being so lazy and write!

Happy Rawan

That night, Rawan sleeps as though she hasn't slept for a long time. Happy and calm, she thinks, *It doesn't matter if we don't have money. The most important thing is that we stick together as a family. I'm so happy. Thank you, God.*

GHADY'S DECISION

ONCE SCHOOL IS OVER, Ghady goes to the front gate to wait for his mom. There, he sees his sister waving and calling to him: "Ghady, wait. Tell me everything! Now. Everything." When Zeina gets close enough, she whispers, breathing hard. "Everybody is talking about the fight. What happened? Who started it?"

"I'll tell you at home. And don't mention it in front of Mom . . . There she is."

But as soon as his mom catches sight of him, she yells. "What are those scratches on your cheek? And why are your clothes so dirty?" The car starts off toward home, but Ghady doesn't say anything. Then, in a barely audible voice, he says, "It was just a little fight, Mom. Don't worry about it."

"And since when do you get into fights?" his mom asks. "What happened?" Her anxiety is showing, and she moves twitchily as she drives.

"Nothing," he says in a faint voice. Then unwanted tears start flowing from his eyes.

"Leave it, Mama," Zeina cuts in. "We'll talk at home."

Ghady's mom and dad listen as he tells them what happened at school. He repeats what he told the principal. He doesn't say anything about how Michael pressured him to buy marijuana. He talks only about Michael's racism and how he constantly provokes him.

Ghady's parents are flummoxed by what their son says about the fight. On the one hand, they're proud of him—instead of running away from conflict, he defended himself against this bully. But on the other, they don't think that problems can be solved with violence, and they don't want to encourage him to use it. Ever. "It was nice of the principal to forgive you this time, Ghady. I hope this is the last time you get in a fight. There are always ways to solve things with words."

Ghady feels a sharp pang, as though a shout of laughter might force its way out if he doesn't hold on tight. *Solve it with words?* he thinks, but he says nothing. *What world are you living in, Dad? Don't you know the laws of the playground are totally different from the world of your preachy advice?*

After his mom finishes tending to the scratches and red-and-blue marks all over his skin, Ghady retreats to his room and stretches out on his bed. While their mom is busy with dinner, Zeina takes the opportunity to slip into her brother's room.

"You have to tell Mom and Dad, Ghady. This is really dangerous—I know Michael's friends, because one boy in my class is friends with him. They're the ones who buy his weed. I mean, God knows where he's getting it."

Ghady thinks Zeina's right. Things are getting worse, and he doesn't know what will happen after today's fight, or what Michael has in mind. Michael is a kid who wouldn't be afraid of doing something really serious. But now, Ghady's exhausted.

"Not tonight, Zeina. I'm really tired, and I still have English homework."

Once Ghady is alone, he turns on the computer and writes to Rawan.

Wednesday, March 10, 2009.

My dear friend,

First, I want you to forgive me for taking such a long time to write back. You should know I haven't changed. And don't worry, I haven't drowned in the rain or been buried under the snow. I'm still the same Ghady you've always known, except I've been really preoccupied. I don't know what to do any more. I have news, but you won't like it. I hope you won't get mad or think bad things about me. You know I was having problems with some of the kids at school, right? And you know about bullying? That's what this boy is doing to me . . . I can't even stand to use his name. He's been pressuring me to buy weed from him at school. He and his friends sell it to other kids. I

95

refused to buy, so he poured all his anger out on me. I wasn't afraid of him, and I stood up to him, but of course he didn't like that . . . which led to this intense fight today. But don't worry about me. Yours truly is pretty strong and muscular. ☺ Some scratches and bruises that will fade is all.

Zeina says I should tell my dad, but I'm not sure. My parents might be tempted to get involved, and, if they do, it will probably make things even worse. What do you think? I know you have enough problems, but you're my best friend, and I can't hide this from you any longer. And by the way, why are you so happy, my dear friend? Is it because of your secret admirer? Did you find out who he is? Is it someone in your class? Come on, tell me! ☺ Do you still want my opinion?

Yours,
Ghady

In the morning, Ghady goes to school, one step forward and ten steps back, as the saying goes. The first thing he notices is Michael, together with Andy, Thomas, Larry, and Sam. They're whispering. Pointing at him. Throwing looks at him. The harshest glances come from Michael. It makes Ghady even more nervous. He doesn't know what's going to happen, but he can feel the pulse of danger.

A NEW DAY

RAWAN OPENS HER eyes in the morning and scans her whole room, smiling. She stares at the stuff in there as if she's seeing it all for the first time. She feels a great joy flood her heart. Before, the intense worry had blinded her, so she couldn't really see what was in front of her. She'd forgotten what her favorite things looked like— her curtains that were a color she'd picked out herself or the plant on her windowsill that had grown and sprouted leaves. Kumari must have been watering it.

In her mind, Rawan returns to how things were before and feels as though she'd been living a nightmare. For a moment, she freezes. A crazy idea takes shape in her head. Could what her dad told them yesterday be a dream? The family meeting that washed away her worry—did it really happen? Rawan jumps up from her bed in terror, runs towards the door and quietly opens it. She peeks out through the crack in the door, looking towards the living room. She sees her parents drinking coffee, chatting, their faces peaceful and at ease. She closes the door and grins widely. She says to herself, *Thank God, it wasn't a dream, it's real. Things are back to the way they were. Now I can focus on school and on figuring out who this mysterious secret admirer is.*

Rawan gets dressed, softly singing the lyrics to an old song her grandma always repeated when she was happy, "Life is sweet, we've just got to live it . . . " She misses her grandma so much. She will visit her soon.

Rawan walks into the schoolyard, her steps light and quick, as if she's hopping. She heads towards the meeting spot with her friends and shouts, smiling, "Good morning, best friends ever! I've missed you all so much." Noor's eyebrows shoot up, surprised. Her gaze meets Rawan's, and she sees Rawan smiling at her. Noor seems astonished, wondering about the reason for this sudden change. Raed looks at Rawan and is taken aback as well. The Rawan in front of him today isn't the Rawan of yesterday. "Don't you guys see that someone who's been missing for a long time has finally come back?" he asks.

"For surrre . . . .we see that," they all respond.

"Don't be so hard on me, Raed. You guys, come on," Rawan says. "I was here all along, I've just gotten better lately. That's all there is to it."

"Totally, but you weren't the Rawan we know. The worrywart Rawan was with us," Raed says. "The gloomy Rawan."

"The negative and desperate Rawan, a real drama queen in every sense of the word," Maya adds.

"The boring and annoying Rawan," Karen chips in. Rawan looks expectantly at Noor, ready to hear her two cents, but Noor doesn't say anything and is just content with a smile.

Laughing, Rawan says, "And who told you guys *that* Rawan is gone? She's still in the building. I can still annoy you all, my best friends ever! Today, I'm the happiest person in the world. I'm happy . . . . so happy." She runs and flaps her arms over and over as if she's flying. "Happy . . . . so happy . . . . HAPPPPYYYY." Her movements catch the attention of the other students, as well as the principal, who looks surprised and can't hold back a chuckle.

That day, Rawan feels energy surge through her veins. In class, she takes part in activities and makes her usual witty comments. In P.E., she jumps, runs, dives for the volleyball, and sends it back with such energy that the P.E. teacher says, "Wow, Rawan, what happened to you? You remind me of Popeye when he eats his spinach. Where is this power coming from? Welcome to the Rawan who never gets tired!"

During the first break, Rawan presents her friends with juice and *mana'eesh* to celebrate her new state of being. She also gives a piece of *mana'eesh* and a juice box to Husam, who she happens to come across in the schoolyard.

Husam is surprised. "What's the occasion, my friend?"

"A new compensation for the accident," Rawan jokes. "Have you already forgotten?"

"Awesome. I wish I could crash into you every day so you'd surprise me with your tasty compensations."

It's got to be him who's been sending me all those gifts. But what is he waiting for? When will he tell me? She moves away from him, distracted, making her way back to her friends under the oak tree.

"Thanks for the food, even though your transformation is worth a bigger meal, say a pizza for example, or a hamburger, or, at the very least, peas and rice," Maya suggests. Everyone laughs.

"I'll make sure to do that and to invite you all as soon as possible to a delicious lunch. But right now, I need to save money. It's all about *taqasshuf.*"

"What does *taqaffush* even mean?" Karen asks. "It's the first time I've ever heard of it."

Raed guffaws, putting on his best French accent. "But of course, Mademoiselle Karen, your mother is zhe French, and your Arabic is zhe broken! *Taqasshuf* means belt-tightening, to keep an eye on your money, you know?" Karen giggles as she repeats, "*Taq . . . shuf . . . Taqasshuf.*"

Rawan tells her friends about her dad. She stretches the truth a little by saying that he chose to leave his job, which is why she has to keep an eye on her spending. Until he finds a new job, she can't ask him for money.

"Oh, that must be so tough!" Maya laments. "To look after your money. I always just ask my mom for money and she gives me whatever I want."

"I'm the opposite, actually," Raed counters. "I always save some money from my allowance, because I rarely eat out. Like my mom says, everything tastes better at home. Don't get upset now, Rawan. Yes, I ate all the *mana'eesh* you gave us and drank the juice. But the ones my mom makes smell so much better, and fresh orange juice is healthier. Today, I sacrificed my butter and apricot sandwich for your sake, my friend."

Karen interrupts, saying that her cousin works in a supermarket near their house in France during the holidays to make extra money. She says most people their age make money by doings small jobs like cutting grass, babysitting, tutoring, or even delivering newspapers in the early morning.

"Me? Work in a supermarket?" Noor asks. "I could never do such a thing. Or take care of naughty children, or work in a garden? No, no, I'll never do such things, and I hope I'm never forced to do them in my life."

"I actually like working. I always help my dad out in the garden at our cabin in the mountains," Raed says. On it goes, back and forth, until the bell rings, announcing the start of classes once again. Rawan decides to think of a way to make her own allowance. She likes what Karen said. *What's wrong with me doing a job suited to my age and getting some cash for it? It's nothing to be ashamed of.*

On her way home, she approaches an old woman who stands on the street corner every day, selling gum and other sweets. This woman is always standing in the same place with a sad look in her eyes. Today, Rawan decides to give her some money. She puts her hand in her pocket and takes out all her change, putting it in the old woman's box and saying, "Here you go. I hope this small amount is enough for you to buy a meal today."

The old woman looks at Rawan and says, "May God protect you from poverty, my girl. May God brighten all your days, just as you've lit up mine." Rawan goes on walking, the woman's prayer following her. *Poor woman. A woman of her age should be resting, getting everything she needs without being forced to stand on the street corner.*

Rawan continues on her way home, feeling lighter, with a smile on her face. What's happened in the last few weeks has changed her, helping her see things from a new perspective.

UNSAFE AT SCHOOL

MICHAEL IS SURROUNDED by all these boys, but who are Ghady's friends? Daniel, who lives in the world of novels, and Charlotte and Liza, who he wouldn't want to involve in the showdown with Michael. And Matthias. Matthias . . . Ghady looks around in search of Matthias. Sees him. He's playing basketball. Ghady waits until Michael and his group lose interest in him for a second, their attention flickering off. Then he heads over. He whispers to Matthias, whose body jumps.

"Come with me. Now. We're going to the principal's office. We have to tell her everything."

"You're crazy," Matthias whispers. "What if one of them sees us? That will be the end of us."

"You have to come with me." Sweat is making hair clump around Ghady's face in ringlets, even though it's cold, and a light snow has started to fall.

"But one of them could see us," Matthias says. "Then we'd be in even worse trouble."

"Yeah, we're already in trouble. Come on, let's not waste time."

Ghady waits a few seconds while Matthias is making up his mind. "Are you coming with me or am I going alone?"

Matthias hesitates a few seconds. "I'm coming."

As soon as Ghady and Matthias step into the principal's office, the situation feels very serious, especially after yesterday's fight. She asks them to come in, and she listens to everything they have to tell her.

Ghady gives details of the boys' threats, and Matthias explains how he caved under their constant pressure.

"I'm worried," Ghady says, finishing up. "And I don't feel safe at school."

"Write me a list of the students' names," the principal says, "and we'll call all of them in."

Before Ghady walks out of the office with Matthias, he turns and tells her: "Please don't tell them we were the ones who said something."

"Don't worry, Ghady. I promise. I won't mention your name, ever."

But oh, their luck . . . ! Just as they come out, they spot Larry. They dash to hide themselves, but he already heard everything from behind the office door.

"See Ghady?" Matthias whispers in a shaky voice. "I was sure they were watching us. What are we going to do now? Why did I let you drag me in here?"

"Don't be scared. We can't let them think we're weak and afraid. Let's go to class. The period's started."

On the playground, just as Ghady expects, Michael's friend Sam comes up to him. "Walk with me. Michael wants a word with you. In the same place, behind the building."

Ghady doesn't want to look scared in front of Michael or his group, so he goes with Sam. But there, behind the building, he sees a much bigger group than the one that usually surrounds Michael. He even sees kids from eleventh grade, from his sister Zeina's class. As Ghady gets closer, his stubborn feet refuse to move any farther. When he's just a short way off, the oldest and biggest boy swoops in. He pushes down Ghady's head, wraps an arm around his neck, and tightens his grip with all his strength. The boys around him call out in encouragement.

"Teach him a lesson!"

"He's got to learn not to snitch."

"I'll break your nose and teeth," the tall, broad-shouldered boy says. "But not at school."

Ghady tries to pull free of the boy's savage grip, but he isn't strong enough. Then he hears a voice. "Look. My friend Frank's ready at any moment. There is definitely going to be hell to pay. But go now, and think about this lesson of the teeth and the nose."

A knife flashes in someone's hand, brightening in the sun, which is beating down and turning the snow even whiter. It's the kind of knife Scouts use at summer camps, and Ghady goes cold from their threats and intimidation. The beast lets him go, and Ghady hears Michael say:

"*Someone* told the administration. The principal sent a message that she wants to talk to each of us individually. So who ratted us out?"

"Who do you think?" Thomas says. "Of course it was Ghady."

"I didn't tell her everything," Ghady says, hoping the boy who grabbed his hand will ease his grip.

"A rat and a liar too? Bravo!" the beast shouts. "That *is* a shame." He raises his hand and gives Ghady's cheek a stinging smack.

"Get out of here now, snitch, with your dirty teeth and your Arab nose."

Ghady runs as fast as he can to get away. He goes right into the principal's office and pushes the door shut behind him with all of his strength. The principal leaps up off her chair.

"What's going on? What's wrong?"

Ghady wheezes. He can't speak.

"Come and sit." The principal gets him a glass of water. Ghady drinks. He heaves a sigh before he starts to speak. After he's reeled off the details, the principal sends her assistant to get Matthias, in fear of the boys and their knife. Ghady is afraid for Matthias too, not only because of Michael and his group, but also because of the principal. After all, Matthias bought weed from Michael, and he smoked it on school property.

"I want the names of all those students, Ghady," the principal says, interrupting his thoughts.

"I don't know the names of all the ones in the older grades," Ghady says, as Matthias steps into the office with the assistant. The principal turns on her computer and asks Ghady and Matthias to pick out photos of the boys who were there. Ghady points to some of the photos, and his friend backs him up, adding the names of two students Ghady didn't know were involved. And so they get to a list of fifteen.

The principal lifts the receiver and asks for Ghady's home number.

"Manal? I'm going to need you to come to school immediately for a very serious matter."

After that, she calls Matthias's house.

"Phyllis? Please come immediately to the school. It's a very serious matter."

Less than fifteen minutes later, Ghady's mom is there, hair un-combed, still wearing her paint-spattered clothes, a coat thrown over them and buttoned up in a hurry. The principal tells her what has been going on, concluding: "It's better if your son stays at home for a while—he's not safe here right now."

After they talk for about a half an hour, the principal sends her assistant to get Ghady's things from his classroom. They decide he should go straight home with his mom. He'll stay away from school, as she suggested, and the principal will call them when they find a solution to the serious problems unfolding on school grounds.

Now that Ghady's mom has found out all the details about the bullying and the pressure he's been under, he's shocked by her reaction. He didn't expect her to be calm. He thought she'd lose it when she heard the word "drugs" and shout, "How could this happen at one of the best schools in Brussels!" But here she is, dealing with it rationally, not forgetting to thank the principal for protecting Ghady, and for letting her know what was going on. She doesn't blame him for not telling her everything, either. She says she's just happy he is safe.

At home, after this packed day, Ghady has to rest. His head aches, and his thoughts are muddled. He goes to his room and shuts the door behind him. He lays down on his bed, closes his eyes, and tries to sleep. But he fails. How can he sleep when his mind is churning with all these stories from school? He decides to send an email to Rawan. He really needs her gentle and encouraging words.

Thursday, March 11, 2009

My dear friend Rawan,

I don't know if you read yesterday's message. I'm your friend Ghady, who lives in a faraway country across the sea, remember me? ☺ . . . I haven't gotten a note from you. Is there a problem with your computer, or, I don't know, maybe you haven't checked your email? Honestly, I've started to hate this place for so many reasons, and the biggest is the atmosphere at school. It really scares me, and anyway I told you about it in the last message.

I really miss Lebanon, and I'm counting down the days until our next visit. My dad booked our tickets for June 30! It's so long to wait, I know. But the time will go fast, my friend.

I'm okay. Tell Jad I have a lot of news for him the next time we meet. These are secrets that stay between the three of us. Promise?

Best wishes,

Ghady

MOUNTAIN HOME

HOW WONDERFUL it is for things at home to go back to how they were! Even Kumari seems happier. Rawan once again enjoys chatting with her parents and Rani over lunch. She puts a mouthful of rice and spinach in her mouth, nibbles at a tasty radish, and laughs, remembering what her P.E. teacher had said. *What are these coincidences? First the peas, and now the spinach!*

Rani tells them that he will work as a part-time receptionist in the gym where he trains in the evenings, so that he can go to classes in the daytime. His work will be answering the phones and responding to customers' questions about the sports programs at the gym.

"There's no need to work, Rani. I'm sorry that I told you to find a job in a moment of anger," their dad says. "The last thing I want is for you to fall behind in your classes. Yes, it's true that I'm unemployed for now, but I'll find something soon. I've put in job applications with several companies. The problem is time. Rest assured, we'll figure it out."

"Darling, there's no need to worry if Rani takes on some responsibility. It will do him good. He has a lot of free time this year, and he can make better use of it."

"Yes, Baba, I think it will be good for me. And I'm thinking about putting in an application to work somewhere on campus next semester. Whatever I earn will be deducted from my fees. My friend Tariq does it—he works a few hours a day in the college library."

"That makes me really happy. Here I thought you were spoiled, but today you proved that you can rely on yourself and shoulder responsibilities," their father says. Rani smiles, proud of the compliment their father has paid him. "In any case, we've decided to sell the mountain house if we have to. We'll get a good chunk of cash from that."

"What?" Rawan shouts. "Our beautiful cabin in the mountains? No Baba, I beg you. Our best summer memories are up there. Please don't sell it." Rawan's parents exchange looks. They hadn't expected her to react like this.

"We'll do anything to save money. We'll cut down on phone calls, we'll keep an eye on how much electricity we use, and we'll cut down on unnecessary purchases. Rani and I will both help you with anything and everything, but we don't want to lose the vacation house. Right, Rani?"

Rani nods slowly, staring at his sister's face in astonishment. He didn't know his little sister could think like this. All this time, he'd underestimated and made fun of her. He looks at the phone in the corner, wondering if he can really cut down on calls to friends as Rawan has suggested. He thinks, *This is going to be hard, but at least I've got to try.*

Rawan's father gets up, steps towards her, and hugs her. "Don't worry, sweetie. Don't be sad. We won't think about selling it anymore. I didn't know it meant this much to you, especially since we only spend a short time there every year."

"That's true, but the short time with our neighbors and friends up there is special, especially with Ghady and Jad," Rawan says, smiling.

Rawan is relieved that her parents agreed not to consider getting rid of their summer getaway. She decides to write to Ghady. She wants to check up on him and see what's going on with him and that gang of troublemakers at school. She also wants to give him all her updates. She can't just tell him all her problems and then not share once they've been resolved. And she still wants his advice about Husam. Should she ask him about the gifts or not? Ghady will definitely give her the best advice.

Rawan boots up her computer. She logs onto her email and starts to read Ghady's message, but then hears the phone ringing. She picks up the receiver, "Hello . . . ?" A woman's voice responds, "Hello, can I speak to your father please?" Rawan falls silent for a moment, then asks, "May I ask who's calling?"

"It's Siham, a colleague from work." Rawan realizes that she recognizes the voice. It's the voice of the woman her dad was talking to that day! She sets down the receiver and makes her way to her parents' 107 bedroom. She finds her father lying down with his eyes closed. *He's sleeping, but I've got to wake him up. I've got to know right now why that woman is calling him.*

Rawan coughs lightly. Her father opens his eyes, which are still clearly heavy with sleep. Before he can say a word, she picks up the receiver from his bedside and holds it out to him. "Phone call for you, Baba," she says. Rawan makes it seems as though she's preoccupied with fixing the alignment of three small pictures hanging on the wall when she's actually hanging on every word her father says.

"Yes . . . Hi Siham, how are you? Fine thanks, I was just lying down. No, I hadn't drifted off completely just yet. How's everyone? No . . . No, I've told them . . . The opposite actually, I wish I would've done it from the start, because things are so much better now, and I'm more at ease . . . Thanks for checking up on me . . . How's your family? Yes, we've definitely got to meet up soon, so we can introduce our families to each other. Tell everyone I say hi. I'll come drop by the office soon . . . Bye then, thanks for calling."

Rawan's dad tries to put the receiver back in place with his eyes half-closed, heavy with sleep. Rawan rushes to him, helps him put it back, and then plants a big kiss on his cheek. His eyes flutter back open, surprise written on his face.

"Baba, I love you so much, and I'm so sorry because . . . because I . . . uh . . . woke you up. Go back to sleep and I won't bother you again." Rawan leaves the room dancing with joy. *How dumb can I be? I made a snap judgment, tortured myself for weeks, and was unfair to Baba because of a misunderstanding . . . And I also destroyed my favorite sweater! Really stupid.*

She sits at her desk reading her email. "Two emails from Ghady at once? Wow!" She reads them eagerly, and then starts her response.

March 18, 2009

Dear Ghady,

This time, I'm the one who's taken so long to respond, although still not as long as you.

What's this you're telling me? I'm worried now, because it seems like things have gotten worse. You're fighting? Like, hitting others and being hit? They're putting pressure on you to buy weed? I can't believe stuff like that happens in your school. What you're telling me sounds like the stuff from gang movies. I hear about things like that happening in a few schools here, but it doesn't sound nearly as dangerous. Stay away from them, Ghady, and tell me you're okay. Try not to hang out with them or get into another fight. Remember what happened last time?

I'm much better now after I found out why Baba was acting different. He told us he lost his job, and everyone felt so much better once he admitted it. The crazy, worrying ideas I had in my head disappeared, since there wasn't an ounce of truth to them. Think about it, Ghady. So I thought he didn't care about us anymore because of his supposed relationship with a woman who wasn't my mom? I discovered today that she's his colleague from work. She was just calling to check up on him.

I thought I might work to earn some money. What do you think?

Unfortunately, my secret admirer is still unknown, even though I'm pretty sure it's Husam, this ninth grader. I always bump into him, but so far he hasn't said anything about the gifts. I still want to know what you think. Should I ask him or wait it out? Won't you tell me what you think? ☹

Hurry up and write back.

Your friend,
Rawan

P.S. I'm happy that you guys have already bought your tickets for the summer!

IN THE HOUSE

GHADY IS HAPPY with the principal's decision—it's sweet to stay safe at home! But this feeling doesn't last long. Soon, he starts getting calls from Michael and his group. Each time one of them calls, Ghady answers. Then they say a few quick things to scare him before he hangs up.

"Are you hiding like a mouse, coward?"

"We'll get our revenge."

"Your teeth aren't going to last very long."

That isn't all—Ghady also gets nasty email messages full of ugly ideas. When Ghady's parents find out about the threatening phone calls, they tell him to stop answering the phone, period. And when he tells them about the emails, his dad prints out copies and keeps them, just in case things get to the point where they need to bring these letters to the police.

"The police?" Ghady asks, when he hears about his father's decision.

In fact, the principal soon calls, asking Ghady's mom and dad to bring him to her office along with any evidence that the boys intend to harm him. The police are already there, writing a report. Ghady and his parents take the threatening messages straight to the school.

In the office, the police ask Ghady a hundred and one questions. He tells them everything he knows and everything he's heard on the playground, then points to pictures of the eleventh-grade boy who threatened to break his teeth and nose. They ask what he knows about Matthias.

"Matthias was really afraid when they threatened him, so he bought marijuana from them once, for twenty euros."

"We'll talk to him, too," one of the officers says.

"He will have to take responsibility for his actions, Ghady," the principal says. "Even if he did it because he was afraid of them. But his punishment will be light, because he came with you and told us what was going on."

All of this has gotten really serious. The *police?* There are three of them: muscular, with big boots, and guns strapped to their sides. Ghady isn't exactly worried about them, but it feels like he's in a movie. Of course, he's one of the good guys.

How did things go so far? Michael is seriously crazy. And the boys who follow his every command . . . the older boys who follow him! As Ghady thinks about them, he also thinks about Matthias. He's worried about Matthias—he definitely doesn't deserve to be punished.

After another week at home, Ghady's mom gets a call from the principal. It's a long call, and Ghady can see anxiety twitching across his mom's face. When she finally puts down the phone, Ghady asks: "What is it? Why are you so pale?"

"That was just your principal, telling me about how the investigations are going. Don't worry about it."

"Is it going to be over soon?"

"I don't think so, sweetie. It seems like this is bigger than we'd imagined. The boys you told us about are backed by a dangerous gang of older guys outside the school. They were using the boys to lure students into experimenting with drugs, then buying."

"And once they got used to it, they couldn't stop," Ghady says.

"Exactly. They'd get addicted. I'm so proud of you."

"Why? I mean, I made a lot of problems for myself when I got involved and told the principal."

"No, the opposite. You did the right thing, sweetheart."

Ghady understands his mom's point of view, but he still wishes he hadn't gotten involved.

"You stopped these guys from getting hold of kids, and not just in your school. I'm sure they were trying to find more stupid boys like Michael to do their business."

Ghady finally feels the seriousness of it all. "When am I going back to school?"

"That's what the principal and I were talking about. We're going 111 to wait a little longer. It might be a month, or it might be more. I suggested you do your schoolwork at home until things are clear. Your teachers will email you the lessons, and then they'll expect you to do the assigned readings and complete any homework they send you."

Once Ghady is back in his room, he thinks about everything that's going on. For sure Michael—plus the dealers who backed him up—will want to get their revenge on him for exposing them. Even if he doesn't go back to school, he still can't leave the house. He'll be too afraid of meeting someone who wants to hurt him.

Then a brilliant idea flashes into Ghady's head. *Why not go to Lebanon now instead of waiting till summer? Since I'm going to school over email, I could do it anywhere. Plus, I would get to see my friends there. Rawan . . . and Jad! I've missed them so much! And Rawan's birthday is soon. April 16. She'll be so happy if I come and celebrate with her.*

Ghady runs to share this amazing idea with his mom.

"It's a good idea, Ghady. Let me talk to your dad when he gets home tonight, and then we'll decide."

SPECIAL DRAWINGS

SEVERAL DAYS go by, and Rawan doesn't get a gift from her secret admirer. Every day, she searches her jacket pockets, her bag, and her desk. She tries not to be affected by it, since she doesn't want to be dragged down or worried about anything from now on. Maybe her secret admirer is trying to save money, just like her.

Rawan devotes herself to her studies, paying particular attention to her art classes. Since the beginning of the year, she has been practicing how to draw on glass, small mirrors, fabric, and wood. She prefers coloring in figures instead of drawing with a pencil or a piece of charcoal. With each passing day, she discovers how much of a master she is at mixing colors.

One day, while supervising her work, the art teacher says, "Your paintings are beautiful, Rawan. You're really good at choosing colors and coordinating them. Your work is thoughtful and exact. There's no doubt you have a bright future as an artist! I've chosen a number of your pieces to be in the end-of-year exhibition. Usually, I choose only one piece per student, but you deserve to have more than one of your works on display."

Rawan is over the moon about this feedback. These few words of encouragement are enough to fire her up to take her art even more seriously. She thinks: *Why not prepare a few pieces and display them in the handicraft exhibition that her mother helps organize every year for charity? If some of them are sold, then she will be playing her part in helping the needy who benefit from the profits of the exhibition. This way, people will get to know her work, and maybe, in the future, she'll get some money out of it.*

Rawan's mom likes the idea and encourages her to pursue her project on the condition that it doesn't affect her grades. "It looks like we're going to have a famous artist in the family! My father, God rest his soul, used to love drawing and painting. There's no doubt you got all your talent from him."

The next day, during the first break, Rawan tells her friends about her idea. "Awesome!" Karen exclaims. "I've always loved your work, and I saw some of it in the art hall. Maybe I'll ask you to whip up some small gifts for my relatives in France. They love everything handmade, especially art from the East. What do you think, Rawan? You'll save me the trouble of having to find them gifts."

"I would love to!" Rawan gushes. "This is a chance for the French people to get to know my work."

"I'm your first customer. Remember that when you become rich and famous," Karen says. "I'm the one who got your work to France in the first place."

Rawan laughs as she turns to Noor and sees her smiling. She inches closer and hugs her, saying, "I'm sorry about what I said that day, Noor. You're my friend and I don't want to lose you. I never congratulated you for being elected class representative, even though that seems like a lifetime ago now. In any case, congrats! You're doing a really great job."

Noor puts her hand on Rawan's shoulder. "Thanks, Rawan. I'm also sorry for sharing your secret, but honestly I just wanted to help, and I didn't mean to hurt you."

"There's nothing better than two friends making up. This whole thing really got to me," Maya says. Then she adds, jokingly, "I think I'm going to cry."

"Where's Raed? I haven't seen him since the start of break," Rawan says, trying to change the subject.

"He must be busy . . . maybe he's at the library returning an overdue book. He mentioned it this morning," Maya says. As soon as she finishes, Raed comes over in a rush.

"Did you return your book, Raed?" Rawan asks. "I hope you didn't have to pay a late fine. Miss Nada the librarian is so strict. For her, a late book is like some kind of unforgivable sin."

Raed is confused. "Book? Which book? I don't have any book." Maya interrupts and gives him a hard look. "Raed, didn't you tell me that you were going to the library to return a book? Think about it."

"Ah . . . yes, the book. Of course . . . Yes, I was in the library. I forgot. How weird that I forgot so quickly."

Rawan notices his face going red and wonders why he and Maya are tripping over their words and contradicting each other. She also sees how concerned Karen and Noor are while Raed is talking. She means to ask what is going on, but then the bell rings, so she makes a mental note to ask during their second break.

Rawan enters class, her head pulsing with thoughts. Are her friends hiding something?

During class, she watches her friends like a hawk: sometimes Karen exchanges looks with Noor, while at other times with Maya. Raed avoids her gaze a few times, and Maya exchanges some signals with Karen.

Rawan wonders what on earth is going on, but she decides to act as though everything is fine and to not bring it up with her friends. She doesn't want to stir up anything else. She knows they love her. She'll just wait until they tell her on their own what is happening—if there even is anything worth mentioning. Maybe there's nothing, and she's just being paranoid.

During the second break, everything goes back to normal, and Rawan starts telling her friends about how she baked a cake yesterday and forgot to add sugar. She describes the expressions on her mother's, father's, and brother's faces when they tasted it.

"Maybe you can put some apricot jam on it. That will make it sweeter and give it some taste," Raed suggests. He stops abruptly and looks over at Karen, Maya, and Noor. He looks like a deer in the headlights. Rawan again ignores what she sees and rushes to change the subject. She plans to figure out what is going on, but at the right time.

At home, when Rawan goes in her room, she looks at her face in the mirror for a long time. She notices that her skin has improved and that her pimples have receded a lot. Her face is calm and radiant.

She splays out on her bed for a bit, thinking of Husam. She hasn't come across him for several days now. Maybe he's absorbed in his work because exams are close. She remembers exams. She opens her bag and stuffs her hand inside to get her science textbook. When she's pulling out her book, she hears a strange rustle. She looks inside her bag. There, she finds a colorful nylon bag. She opens it and looks inside. She freezes for a moment, then her face lights up with a big grin. She says to herself, *Now I know who my secret admirer is.*

She lies back down on her bed and thinks. She starts to laugh. Her laugh gets louder and louder until her mother opens her bedroom door. "Rawan, what on earth is happening? What's making you laugh like this?"

Still doubling over, Rawan says, "Don't worry Mama, I'll tell you later. I promise. Don't worry."

Her mother insists that Rawan tell her, but Rawan keeps promising that she'll tell her soon, really soon. That afternoon, Rawan goes to the store next to her house to buy some of the tools that she'll need. Back in her room, she works late into the night and falls asleep, impatient for the next day . . . It better come soon.

HERO

ON AN AFTERNOON that Ghady spends mostly in front of the TV, he gets a call from Matthias. Ghady's life is now like this: TV, Playstation, Internet, playing the oud, and a little bit of studying . . .

"Hey Matthias. What's up?"

"Big things are happening. The whole middle and high school are talking about the drug deals. And today, the administration sent home something to the parents. It said they caught the guys responsible for pushing drugs to the boys who were selling at school."

"Did they give names?"

"No, but everyone in class is sure that Michael and Frank and Gabi are the leaders."

Frank was the one who had the knife, and Gabi was the beast who attacked and threatened him. Just hearing their names makes Ghady feel queasy. He is still afraid of them getting their revenge.

"It's a lot for you," Ghady says. "Michael pushed you around. I mean, doesn't the administration know the difference between you and the guilty ones?"

"We'll see. The principal said I should come to her office tomorrow so she can tell me my punishment. Anyway, I had to speak up, because I was scared for you. Oh, hey—me, Daniel, Charlotte, and Liza are going downtown Saturday afternoon, and we want you to come with us. We miss you, and it's really sad not having you at school."

"Nah, I don't think I can go out. What if I run into Michael or Larry or one of those guys?"

"Okay. What if we meet at Daniel's? For sure he'll be happy. It's not a good idea to meet at my house—you know I live next to Michael. I'll talk to Daniel and the girls. Saturday at five. Okay?"

"That's a great idea. I'll go ask my mom."

Ghady is excited at the thought of meeting his friends—he's really yearned to see his friends, especially since he's been feeling bored by the long, identical days. His dad is always at work, Zeina is at school, and his mom works part-time, and then comes home to do her drawing or cooking, or else she's out shopping. He's left at home, waiting for everyone. After his mom agrees to let him go to Daniel's, Ghady heads back to the phone.

"Done deal. See you Saturday!"

But what Ghady doesn't expect is that, when he gets to Daniel's house, he's greeted with applause. As soon as he steps into the house, his friends clap as they laugh and chant his name: "Ghady! Ghady!" Then Charlotte pulls out a t-shirt that says: "A Real HERO Always Does the Right Thing." Ghady goes up and hugs each of his friends.

"What's all this?" he asks. "Is this some kind of ceremony?"

"You're a hero, Ghady," Liza says. "Don't you know?"

"You told them the names of those bullies at school, and you saved a bunch of kids from them and the drugs they were pushing."

"It wasn't just me," Ghady says. "I mean, Matthias was with me. So he's a hero too, if you insist on calling it that."

"No way. I couldn't have stood up to Michael and those guys. Plus it was your idea to go to the principal, and you're the one who's paying the price. Nobody's threatening me, since I bought from them once. And they think you forced me to go tell on them. Anyway, my punishment was really small compared to Michael's. I have to do some work in the library during first semester next year—that's it."

"Honestly, after all the threats and everything? I wish I hadn't ever gotten involved. Since I gave their names, I've been constantly worried, every day."

"No way, Ghady, don't regret it," Daniel says. "You have no idea how many kids are talking about you like you're a real hero."

Ghady smiles. What great friends . . . he really loves them!

"Let's go out to the garden. My mom put out juice and cake."

Ghady is filled with joy at being surrounded by these loyal friends. He thinks about Jad and Rawan. The news he has to share with them is really piling up. He has grown up so much in the last few months. Do they feel the same way?

SECRET ADMIRER

RAWAN GETS UP earlier than usual, goes into the kitchen to have her breakfast, and puts together what she'll take to school all on her own.

She gets dressed in a hurry and organizes the stuff in her bag before she heads for the door. That's when her mother appears, surprised. "Rawan, what's happening? Why are you leaving so early today? Where's this sudden burst of energy coming from?"

"I've got something important to do. See you!" She kisses her mom's cheek and rushes out.

Rawan stands alone below the oak tree, waiting for her friends. She really misses them. It's like she's gone back in time. It's as if this is her first day of school—like she's just back from summer vacation, and she can't wait to see each of them after such a long time apart.

Her friends start to arrive. Karen first, then Maya. They're amazed to find Rawan there before them, since she usually arrives after them, even though her house isn't very far. Only a few minutes later, Raed arrives, with Noor behind him. Finally, they're all here.

"I've brought something for you guys," Rawan says. From her backpack, she pulls out a bag, opens it, and takes out pieces of cake covered with apricot jam. She gives them each a slice. "I took your advice, Raed." He nods as he munches his piece, "Mmm . . . yummy." While everyone is trying the cake, Rawan takes a box out of her bag with some hazelnut chocolate pieces, a small white bear, a glass, a beaded bracelet, a card, a colored pen, and finally one jar with a little apricot jam left in it.

Rawan surveys her friends' faces as they take in all the stuff. She sees that their mouths are still full of cake. They exchange glances, then all burst out laughing, the pieces of jam-covered cake flying out of their mouths.

Rawan starts to laugh, too. They all laugh until they cry. After they calm down, each trying to catch their breath, Maya attacks Raed: "It's all your fault! You ruined everything. You gave her apricot jam and then what do you do? You tell her to put apricot jam on her cake. What a strange coincidence, huh?"

"Didn't you like the jam, Rawan? I helped my mom make it."

"I can't even begin to explain how much you all helped me with what you did. I really thank you. I love you guys." Then she goes on, joking, "Even though I was really disappointed to find out there was no secret admirer. I'd started to like the idea, you know?"

"We did it to put you in a better mood," Karen says. "But we never thought you might think you had a secret admirer. Actually, Maya warned us, but we didn't listen to her." Karen turns to Maya and says, "See, you were right, it did happen" Maya then booms, as if she's a commentator at a soccer game, "So from now on, don't ever doubt what Maya says."

Rawan takes a bag out of her backpack. Inside are colored pieces of wood, each of them shaped like a frame, with the picture of a heart inside. Each has written on it "Best Friends," along with each of their names. She gives each of her friends a frame and says, "I drew it, wrote the dedication, and colored it all in one night. You all mean so much to me. You all helped me out in my darkest hour and stood by me. I'll never forget it."

Rawan turns to the schoolyard entrance and sees Husam coming in. She jogs towards him to give him a slice of the jam-covered cake. He smiles. "Thanks, friend. You're always brightening my day with your delicious gifts."

Rawan watches her friends from afar. She'd used Husam as an excuse to get some distance from them, since she's so overcome with emotion she thinks she might cry. She thinks of her friend Ghady. How she misses him and hopes to see him soon! That evening, she writes to him, a big smile on her face.

Thursday, March 26, 2009

Ghady,

To my dear best friend who lives far away, across the seas, in a country where it rains every single day of the year. Today was epic, because I discovered a beautiful truth. I discovered that I'm surrounded by friends who care about me and love me, and who wanted to save me from the sadness I was drowning in. I found out that there's no secret admirer. It was my friends who were sending me those small gifts to put me in a better mood, and they actually did succeed in making me hopeful and happy. Instead of a secret admirer, I discovered that I have dear friends who thought about making me happy and standing by me, without me even realizing it.

I'm waiting for you to come back in June, Ghady, and until then we'll keep emailing. I'll tell you everything that happens to me. I've nicknamed Jad "summer friend" because we barely meet, but we do sometimes talk on the phone. He's well, and he told me two jokes when we talked last time. He also told me he's gotten used to his tons of homework and exhausting exams.

I really can't wait for spring break and have already started planning what I'm going to do. I'm going to make up for all the hard times that I've had. And what are your plans for the break?

Don't take too long to write back.

Your friend who misses you a lot,
Rawan

A GIFT

ON SUNDAY morning, Ghady puts on the t-shirt his friends gave him. While having breakfast with his family, he tells them about his visit to Daniel, and about the news from school.

"We have something to tell you, and I think you'll like it," his dad says.

"What?" Ghady's voice rises. "What is it?"

"You're lucky, brother," Zeina says.

"Get ready," his mom says. "Your trip is coming soon."

Ghady looks around. "My trip to Lebanon? You agreed to it? Am I going alone? When? At what—"

"Take it easy, bud," his dad says. "One question at a time."

"Yes," his mom says. "You'll spend three weeks in Lebanon. The Easter holiday is coming soon, so you can spend some time with your friends."

"You'll go alone," his dad adds. "We've made all the travel arrangements, and you'll stay at your grandparents' in Beirut."

"Did you tell anyone there?" Ghady asks.

"I told your grandma. Why?"

"Because I want to surprise Rawan and Jad."

"Okay," his mom says. "I'll call her now and let her know not to tell them."

"When am I going?"

"Three days from now."

Ghady bolts his breakfast. As soon as he finishes, he runs to the computer.

He turns it on to see if there's anything from Rawan.

There's a new message.

Friday, April 10, 2009

My dear friend Ghady,

I hope you're good, and that the problems you were having with that group of annoying boys are over. I want you to give me all the details, because Rawan is sooo curious and can't wait to hear all the news. ☺

I'm fine, and I miss you, my friend. I heard from Jad that my friends at school are throwing me a birthday party next Thursday. It was supposed to be a surprise, but you know Jad. He called after I hadn't heard from him in such a long time, and as usual he couldn't keep a secret. He asked a bunch of questions about my friends, and I knew right away they had called to invite him. They know we're close. Anyway, I'll pretend to be surprised so they won't get mad at him . . .

I wish you could be with us, Ghady. I feel like I'm really going to miss you on my special day, because I'm going to be with all my closest friends, and only you, my dear friend, will be missing.

Waiting to hear all your news,

Rawan the Curious

Ghady's next thought delights him: he'll surprise Rawan at her birthday party! He'll have to arrange it with Jad when he gets there.

When his traveling day comes, Ghady feels his heart jumping out of his chest. He can't believe he's going to Lebanon in the early spring instead of waiting for summer.

On the plane, he sits next to the window, one row in front of the flight attendants. This is totally different from how he felt going back to Brussels at the end of the summer. Now, his heart leaps in his ribcage, a smile won't leave his face, and thoughts zing around in his mind about what he'll do with his friends in Lebanon: how Rawan will react to his story . . . where he'll go with Jad . . . the sun and the warmth he's missed so much.

From time to time, he checks his pocket to make sure Rawan's present is still there—a silver necklace with a half-heart pendant that has "friends" written on it. He checks his own neck to make sure the other half of the phrase is still hanging there: "forever."